TROPICAL
DREAMS

TROPICAL DREAMS

•

Jillian Dagg

AVALON BOOKS
THOMAS BOUREGY AND COMPANY, INC.
401 LAFAYETTE STREET
NEW YORK, NEW YORK 10003

PRINTED IN THE UNITED STATES OF AMERICA
ON ACID-FREE PAPER
BY HADDON CRAFTSMEN, BLOOMSBURG, PENNSYLVANIA

To my husband, Jim, who supports my dreams.

Chapter One

Silver Island. Rayne Sinclair watched from the window as the small plane swooped closer to the volcanic mound of land that sprouted with lush green foliage and was interspersed with what Rayne called bald spots. The tallest building on the island was the Silver Island Resort Hotel. Three rambling stories of white siding, roofed with flamingo-pink tile. The hotel's offspring cascaded down a hillside, a jumble of pink and blue villa roofs, resembling hats tossed among the trees. At the base of the hillside, protruding into the sea, was a narrow neck of land. On one side lay a silver sand beach, the other, a marina, where the identifying flags or burgees breezily topped the masts of the yachts moored there. It was be-

1

ginning to get dark, and, like fireflies, lights twinkled here and there.

The pilot, Janet Pinkerton, guided the plane down onto a flat piece of land north of the hotel. Only a few flares illuminated the short runway, and the nerves in Rayne's stomach pinched tightly, the way they always did on the abrupt descent. However, she also felt excited to be back after spending Christmas with her parents in Michigan.

Janet, a short brunet in white jeans and windbreaker, hopped out to haul Rayne's luggage off the plane. ''I flew a guy named Nick Lewis in yesterday.''

Janet always chattered when she loaded and unloaded luggage. Part of keeping her passengers feeling calm, Rayne had always supposed. But this chatter Rayne felt was truly directed toward her. It was important. Rayne picked up her navy garment bag and shouldered it. ''Should I know that name, Jan?''

Janet swung another suitcase onto the ground. ''If you're smart, you should. I mean, he arrived as a guest—at least he seemed to want it to appear that way. Yet I happen to know he's Lewis Recreational Enterprises. One of his company's resorts is on St. Thomas. My husband, Bill, has flown Lewis there a couple of times. That's why I'm telling you he's here. If you get my drift.''

Rayne assembled together the rest of her luggage—a suitcase, carry-on, and a quilted bomber jacket, which she had more than needed in Flint—to wait for her nephew Sean to pick her up in the resort's Suzuki. "You mean a warning?" she asked.

"Exactly. According to my Bill, Nick Lewis has been scouting the British Virgins for a long time, looking for a prime spot for another L.R.E. resort. He doesn't build new. He buys established places and fixes them up into luxury resorts."

Despite feeling tired from the long trip, Rayne endeavored to put Janet's information into perspective. "Like Silver Island, for instance?"

Janet nodded. "Possibly."

"Well, he can think twice. I took on the management of Silver Island when my brother died to help Tanya and the boys keep it, not to sell it. After all my hard work, we're certainly not parting with it. If we sold the island, we'd be destroying Larry's dreams. Will you mention that to Nick Lewis when you fly him *off* the island, Janet?"

"I might not get the chance before you tell him yourself. He's staying here for a month."

"A month!"

"That's what Rosie told me."

"If Rosie's been discussing this with you, then I'm presuming this man is news." Rosie was

Rayne's extremely competent assistant, who had a penchant for the juiciest gossip.

Janet straightened the lapels of her windbreaker and grinned. "He's very definitely news. If I wasn't *very* married, I'd give Nick Lewis more than a second look. He's gorgeous, Rayne."

Rayne sighed. "I haven't got time for gorgeous men with alleged agendas. I'll avoid him."

"I doubt if you'll be able to do that. He's one of those men who attracts women without any effort."

Rayne was about to answer that remark, when Janet looked at her watch. "I've got to fly. Another passenger due to be picked up in half an hour. See ya. Don't forget: *no* works."

"Even on guys like Nick Lewis?"

"Let's hope so. I've enjoyed flying to Silver Island since you've been boss."

"That's a nice compliment. Thanks. And thanks for a great flight."

With the velvety tropical breeze rustling her long print dress and lifting her sleek auburn hair, Rayne watched the little plane take off. The buzz of the engine matched the buzz of Janet's words in her head. It wouldn't be the first time someone had tried to buy the island resort. In the past couple of years Rayne had often received letters, and even blatant financial proposals, all of which she promptly tossed into the wastebasket. But she understood the intent of the offers. Silver Island, after all, was prime real estate.

Not that she had the right to make a decision. Although Rayne had invested herself, the bulk of the resort belonged to Larry's wife, Tanya. However, after Larry's death, Tanya really hadn't known how to cope, and it had been Rayne who had rushed to her sister-in-law's side and used her previous corporate administrative experience to take hold of the reins, which Tanya readily relinquished.

Rayne hadn't known that her brother had run Silver Island on a shoestring, and she had to do the same. For a while there were a certain number of return guests; the resort needed constant upgrading and flashy advertising to attract new ones. And, whereas Rayne took a modest salary, Tanya required a substantial income to keep herself in the wealthy style she had been accustomed to all of her life. She was also determined to give her boys the education Larry had planned for them.

Mind you, Rayne thought, as her twenty-two-year-old nephew, Sean, abruptly stopped the red Suzuki beside her, things in the education department were going a little awry at the moment. Justin, the youngest, was on track. He was staying in Flint with Tanya's parents while he completed high school. But Sean, who cut out of college when his father died, never returned, preferring to stay on the island. There was a running battle going on between Tanya and her elder son.

Sean switched off the engine and clambered out, the beam of the headlights reflecting his ear-length fair hair, white shorts, and snug T-shirt. He looked very much like her brother. Too much, sometimes. Rayne had often come upon her nephew and felt her stomach pull with emotion.

Sean gave her a peck on the cheek. ''Hi, Auntie Rayne. Had a good time?''

''Very nice, except it snowed just about every day. I've got lots of gifts from the family for you.''

''You got my CDs I hope.''

''I've especially got your CDs.'' Rayne had spent an entire day in a mall buying from his music list.

''Great. You're the best aunt to have. A young one.''

Rayne laughed and Sean packed her luggage into the Suzuki.

Rayne gripped one side of the topless vehicle as it bumped down the middle of the steep sandy road that was fit more for goats than cars. Sean drove with his foot flat on the gas pedal, and Rayne decided, as always, that landing on the island in the small plane was a placid experience compared to the prospect of her head pitching forth from the bouncing vehicle.

The brakes screeched. Rayne winced. Sean turned the Suzuki into the sharp curve of the circular driveway. Colored lights made the spray sparkle in the fountain and lit up the palmettos gracing the edge of the pathway leading to the hotel, then beamed upwards to the balconies, their white wood columns laced with tangerine blossoms. In daylight, from the balconies, guests had a tremendous view down the hill and over the blue Sir Francis Drake Channel.

Once around the hotel, Sean continued to zigzag the Suzuki down the rest of the hill. The path was smoother here, enabling Rayne to enjoy the musky scent of tropical plants. Ah, it was good to be back.

Sean turned into a narrow lane densely lined on both sides with trees. Along this lane were the larger, most expensive villas. Rayne wondered where Nick Lewis was staying.

"Did you meet a guest named Nick Lewis?" she asked Sean as he stopped the Suzuki outside a white stucco villa. Ship-style lamps shone over the door, the glow settling on the fuchsia hibiscus sprawling up the walls. Purple shutters shaded the windows of her home on the island, Jasmine villa.

"Sure did. I drove him down here yesterday.

We played tennis together last night. He's staying next door to you in Gardenia.''

If Janet's assumptions were correct, Nick Lewis might have positioned himself next door to her for a very good reason. ''Did you say you played *tennis* with him?''

''Yep. He was great. Used to play hockey and football as well. We're considering a trip to another island for a game of golf. Do you know him then, Auntie?''

Sean helped Rayne out of the vehicle in a gentlemanly fashion that impressed her. She thought he did well greeting guests, driving them at a thrilling pace around the resort, and hauling luggage. Maybe that's what he really wanted out of life, to work at the resort his father had put all his energy and dreams into; dreams Rayne fought to keep alive. Dreams Nick Lewis wasn't going to destroy.

Rayne shouldered her garment bag again. ''No, I don't know him. I've just heard about him.''

''You'll probably like him. He's er . . . well, mother says he's a hunk.''

Rayne walked along the sandy path to the villa, Sean following with the rest of her things. The door was open. There were no locks on Silver Island. ''Does your mother know him already?''

''He ate dinner with us last night. I'll introduce you, if you want. Mom keeps saying that we should get you hitched to a nice guy. And she approves of Nick Lewis. By the way, before I forget, Mom said she'll meet you at the Bay View Terrace restaurant in a couple of hours for dinner.''

Rayne tried to reposition her thoughts after all she'd heard about Nick Lewis. He sure seemed to leave an impression on those he met. ''That's fine. I'll be there.''

Sean put down her luggage and flexed the muscles in his arms. ''I'll go tell her.''

''How are you and your mom getting along, Sean?''

''Fine. If we don't mention the word college. You're going to have to change her mind, Auntie Rayne. I want to take Dad's place here.''

''I realize how you feel, Sean. The island's great, but maybe you should finish your education first.''

''I am having an education. *Here*. Doesn't anyone see that?''

Rayne nodded. ''I understand what you mean. It is an education in life, but you still need the formal type.''

''I'm not an academic. I figured that out in the year I was in college. I'm much better at sports and physical stuff. I know I could go to golf school or something like that, but that's not really my scene either.''

Rayne shook her head. ''Your father was the same, a great football player, but a disaster at math.'' Which was probably why the books hadn't balanced when she'd first taken over the office work here. The precarious financial situation at Silver Island was another problem Christmas hadn't erased. Difficulties remained, despite the holiday. And she wasn't about to step on her sister-in-law's toes regarding her son. ''Anyway, Sean, it's your decision, finally, I suppose. Now let me take a shower and relax a little.''

''What about the CDs?''

''Ah, yes.'' Rayne lifted her carry-on bag, unzipped it, and handed Sean the package of CDs. ''That's an extra Christmas gift from me.''

''Great. Thanks, Auntie. See you later.''

''Enjoy them, Sean.''

Sean left with his precious bundle of music from home, and Rayne pushed back her hair to help calm herself down. It was a long trip from Flint. Her surviving brother, George, had driven her to Detroit, from where she'd flown to Miami. There she'd had quite a long wait for a flight to Puerto Rico. From San Juan she'd flown to Beef Island, where, thankfully, Janet had been waiting.

Rayne slipped her feet out of her pumps and rolled off her hose. The cool, pearly tiled floor was a soothing relief to her bare feet.

She loved her villa, which had two bedrooms,

each with its own en suite bathroom, and a small kitchen she rarely used, other than to pare fruit for snacks or serve herself beverages. An overhead ceiling fan slowly whirred above the sitting-room area, wafting a fresh sea breeze through the rooms.

Needing to absorb some more of the sultry scented air, Rayne flung open the French doors that led onto a veranda shaded by a palm-thatched roof, blossom shrubs, and banana trees. Holding on to the railing, Rayne inhaled deeply and gazed downhill toward the marina and the beach.

Beyond the bay, she could make out the bulging shapes of more islands. Tortola was across there, with Virgin Gorda to her right. The British Virgins were an archipelago of islands in a jewel of a sea that Larry had fallen in love with on his first trip here.

Rayne took another deep breath. She'd thought about Larry enough this evening. To snap herself out of her melancholy, she walked to the end of the veranda that overlooked the Gardenia villa.

Nick Lewis's thatched veranda was illuminated by interior lights. Someone was moving around inside the sitting room. Before she could stop herself, Rayne stepped back into her own villa, found the small binoculars that she normally used for spotting boats at sea, walked to the end of the veranda once again, and put the lenses up to her eyes.

The person inside the Gardenia villa opened the doors and walked out. Nick Lewis? Rayne knew she was spying, but the binoculars seemed to be glued to her eyes, for Janet's description didn't do the man justice. Like herself, he was barefoot, wearing a pair of loden green shorts, the kind with pockets, safari style, and a mulberry shade T-shirt. He had muscular, tan legs sparsely covered with a few dark hairs, and solid arms and shoulders. His hair was light brown and thick, accenting dense brows, and what seemed to be keen, alert eyes—she pondered what color they might be. His nose was strong, his mouth nicely curved, humorous . . .

He moved closer to the railing and leaned his folded arms against the top. Then he glanced her way. Almost as if he could sense the binocular lenses trained on him.

Rayne hurriedly removed the binoculars from her eyes and hustled inside. She prayed he hadn't seen her.

Rayne arrived at the trellis entrance of the Bay View Terrace restaurant. At night the lights illuminated glossy-leaved greenery dripping with vibrant-colored blossoms. Young male waiters, wearing black shorts and floral red and blue shirts, trays balanced on upturned palms, moved efficiently under the palm roof between the shiny glass-topped wicker tables.

One of the waiters came over to her. "Hi, Rayne. You're back."

She nodded and smiled. "Yes, Jack, I'm back. I'm . . ."

"Nick Lewis is at the corner table waiting for you."

Rayne's arms were a mass of goosebumps despite the heat. She crossed her arms and rubbed them. "Nick Lewis waiting for me?"

"Yes. He said you were meeting him here."

"No, Jack. I'm meeting Tanya here."

"Mrs. Sinclair's also there."

Rayne glanced over to where Jack indicated. Tanya, wearing a white sundress, her lustrous raven hair spilling around her delicate features, was leaning across the table talking animatedly to the man Rayne had been looking at—she couldn't bring herself to acknowledge that she had actually spied—on the veranda of the neighboring villa.

Still in the same shorts and T-shirt, Nick Lewis lounged in a wicker peacock chair, appearing as if he were meant to be there. Well, he was, in some ways. He'd obviously paid for his month's stay with hard cash, or at least accredited plastic. Except he might have an ulterior motive for being here, a motive Rayne didn't want to hear about. Especially not tonight, during her first few hours back on the island, when she was edgy from the trip. If an inevitable meeting had to come about, she would rather do it after a good night's sleep, *and* from behind her office desk. She wanted to keep it businesslike. Then what had she been doing with the binoculars, an action far from businesslike? And had he seen her? Is that why he was here waiting? Or was Nick on a mission to persuade Tanya?

Her sister-in-law saw her and beckoned. "Rayne, over here!"

Rayne waved to Tanya. She should have stayed in her villa and ordered her meal in.

"Rayne," Tanya was standing up now. "Come on."

Reluctantly, her heartbeat echoing in her head, Rayne wound her way through other tables and made her way to Tanya's side. The two women hugged.

"It's so good to have you back. We missed you terribly at Christmas. It was lonely with only Sean and myself."

Rayne avoided making eye contact with the man watching them. What if he had seen her with her binoculars? "You know you both could have come home with me."

Tanya made a face. ''I can't bear the cold now.''

Rayne nodded sympathetically. Her sister-in-law had suffered a great deal of anxiety since her husband's death. All Tanya's dislikes were mere excuses for the security of staying put. She hadn't left the island since returning from the funeral. Something that worried Rayne. It also worried Rayne that Nick Lewis might be working on that vulnerability.

Tanya kept her arm around Rayne. ''Rayne, this is Nick Lewis. I don't know if you've ever met him before, but he came to stay on the island once before, when . . . Larry . . . was here.''

''I haven't met him.'' Rayne was unsure how she kept her voice steady. ''How do you do . . . Nick.''

Nick Lewis rose from his seat, tall and lean, a perfect specimen of manhood. Close up, more beautiful than at a distance, which was not what Rayne wanted to see. A pockmark or a flabby muscle would have been more acceptable. Just some small imperfection to stop her from feeling floored by his presence.

''Hi, Rayne. How are you?''

His voice was deep, electric, vaguely amused, and when he shook her hand she should have been ready to feel the shivery shock that trembled down her spine. ''I'm fine, thanks.'' She couldn't bring herself to say his name for she knew, by the ferocity of her physical reaction to him, that it would drift out breathless, husky, on a sigh, thus giving him all the wrong connotations.

"Sit down," Tanya urged. "We were waiting on you before we ordered dinner."

Realizing she was doomed to stay with Nick and Tanya, Rayne sat down in another peacock chair and smoothed a magenta flower on the skirt of her cream sundress. "I'm not all that hungry. When I travel I eat everything that is served up, and I stuff myself." A stupid thing to say, she thought.

Nick leaned forward slightly. "Why don't you have something light? Grilled fish, or shrimp, maybe. It's on me."

The last thing in the world Rayne wanted was for Nick to buy her dinner. She was quite aware that she needed to retain the upper hand. "Thank you, anyway, but there's no need. Tanya and I eat gratis. We'll put you on our check."

"If you insist, but I wouldn't want the resort to lose money."

No of course not, Rayne thought. *You want to buy the place.* What a worm he was, the way he had wriggled himself in with her sister-in-law, not to mention playing tennis with Sean. By now he acted as if he had a right to be eating dinner with the owner and the manager of the resort.

These thoughts made Rayne stop feeling embarrassed about looking at him on his veranda. He deserved it.

When Nick rested the sole of one white canvas shoe on the bottom rung of the railing, Rayne didn't let herself look at his powerful athletic legs. She didn't think how those legs might look in white shorts when he was playing tennis. Instead, she read the menu. Grilled fish and a little sweet potato was about all she fancied. She told the waiter that, and then the others gave their orders.

"Wine?" the waiter asked.

"Champagne," Nick said. "The best you have. And put it on my hotel bill."

Tanya's tongue moistened her lips. "Sounds good."

Nick spared a smile for her, even though Rayne felt his attention was now focused solely on her. Did he think he could get further with her than with Tanya?

"So, Rayne," he asked, "did you have a good trip back to the island?"

"Yes. Thank you." She declined to ask how his own trip had been. Let him believe she thought he'd been here for a while and that she had no advance knowledge of his proposed deal. That way he'd think he was conning her. Two can play your game, Nick Lewis!

Tanya laughed. "Now that all those important details are out of the way, let's hear about Christmas, Rayne."

Pleased to have her attention turned away from Nick Lewis, Rayne gave Tanya a brief account of the family Christmas and her visit with Justin, who wouldn't be coming to Silver Island for a few months. "I have gifts from the family for you," Rayne told her. "We'll get together tomorrow evening when I've unpacked."

"It'll be like a second Christmas."

Tanya's expression was that of an excited child, and Rayne was pleased to see her sister-in-law taking more of an interest in life instead of being enshrouded in grief. Maybe this year her life would turn around.

The waiter brought and poured the champagne, the remainder of which was left in an ice bucket on a silver trolley beside Nick.

Nick lifted his glass. "Here's to paradise."

The women raised their glasses to clink with his. After a couple of sips, Rayne felt the bubbles immediately invade her head. The last beverage in the world she needed to drink was champagne. With Nick Lewis across the table, she felt as if she'd imbibed a few gallons already, and cursed herself for reacting so gullibly to a handsome man. Although handsome was too mild a description for Nick. He was the type of man women had dreams about. Janet had been right.

Nick put down his glass. "It must be nice to have a huge family, Rayne."

With his brilliant gaze trained on her—he had the longest lashes Rayne had ever seen on a man—Rayne knew she was going to speak shakily. "Yes. I like it. There's always a support network. Don't you have a big family?"

"No. I was the only child, and my mother and father divorced."

"Are they still alive?" Rayne was surprised at how much she suddenly needed to know about Nick Lewis. And she felt her body language change. Unable to stop herself, she leaned forward, toward him.

"They're very much alive. My father's an engineer and my mother is Christina Theresa Lewis, who writes science fiction under the name C. T. Lewis."

Tanya patted his bare arm. "You're kidding. Rayne reads her all the time. Then she passes her books on to me. We're big fans. Rayne especially."

That was a piece of personal information Rayne wouldn't have readily shared if she'd been alone. She didn't want to appear enthusiastic over anything having to do with Nick Lewis. But, yes, she did love C. T.'s books. C. T. created fascinating utopian worlds, perfect worlds that appealed to Rayne's need for a sense of order. Except the characters in C. T.'s world were always swayed by unbelievable passion and sizzling romance. Her heroes were always wonderful, strong men, who understood their women perfectly; dream men who looked like her son.

Thinking that very thought, she glanced at Nick. "Did your parents ever get married again— to other people, I mean?"

Nick missed a couple of beats before he said, "No, they didn't."

Rayne heard something in Nick's tone that told her that his parents' marital situation didn't please him. Or did it hurt him?

Nick chuckled. "No one can live with mother anyway. She's involved in her writing to such an extent that she's off in another world. She hasn't budged from her Manhattan apartment in years."

"You should invite her here," Tanya told him. "It would be fun to meet a real writer, but then, maybe she doesn't like traveling. I don't. I get sick on boats and scared out of my wits on planes."

"Does that mean you're stranded on this island, Tanya?" Nick observed.

Tanya nodded. "You might say that, but there could be worse places to be stranded. This was my husband's dream island, Nick, and I feel close to him here.''

Nick glanced at Rayne. ''Is that also how you feel?''

Rayne met his gaze head-on. Tanya had unwittingly given Nick Lewis a fantastic answer, therefore she might as well add her two cents' worth. It could make him back off and go home. ''I'm keeping my brother's dreams alive, yes.''

''I see,'' Nick said.

Rayne was sure he did see. She hoped he saw the whole picture. No sale.

Rayne ate her meal quickly. Then, despite protests, she departed the restaurant entertaining thoughts of checking out her office in the hotel to see what correspondence and work had accumulated, but decided against it. Tomorrow would be soon enough to attack the deluge. What she needed now was instant relief from her day's travel, and especially from Nick Lewis.

Therefore, instead of going to her villa, she went to the beach. Although it was dark, beams of light from the resort stretched across the white sand and made it easy to see. At first, still in a hurried, city mode, she walked fast. But as the fresh breeze lazily tousled her hair and shimmied the fabric of her dress around her legs, her footsteps gradually slowed to a more leisurely stroll.

Feeling more serene, she sat down on a rock facing the sea.

Closing her eyes for a second, Rayne felt the soft salty air caress her skin and realized how much she truly loved Silver Island. So much so that there was no way she was going to cave in to Nick Lewis's charm. All a woman needed was distance from a man like him.

Rayne heard soft footsteps on the sand behind her. Rapidly opening her eyes, she glanced around. Nick, standing close to her, was bigger, broader, the muscles in his legs and arms seeming to be coiled with restrained energy.

He looked like a man ready to challenge her as he hunkered down beside the rock until his brilliant gaze was level with hers. "Hi."

Rayne's hammering heart made her aware of his hard-muscled body that was so near now. "Finished dinner already?" she asked shakily. Why couldn't she behave normally with him? And now that they were alone, was he going to mention that he'd seen her looking at him through binoculars? Question her? Ask her about selling the island?

"Yes. Tanya had some things to do, so we didn't linger." There was a twinge of humor in his tone that matched the generous curve of his mouth.

Rayne didn't want to look at him, so she rested

her gaze over his shoulder, on the saltwater swimming pool that was hewn out of a rock basin. "You're quite friendly with Tanya."

Nick shifted his head to one side so that Rayne was forced to look him in the eye again. "Well, we have met once before, but after I arrived, I made friends with Sean, and it seemed natural to join them both for dinner last night. And tonight."

"Such a quick worker!"

"No way."

"Why not? She's pretty."

"Very pretty, but she's quite a bit older than me. Also, she's not over her husband's death yet."

His thoughtfulness astounded Rayne. She had been certain that he would be ruthless, without concern for people's feelings. "You're right."

"Although," Nick went on, "it's not particularly healthy to be in love with a man who's been dead for a number of years."

"You don't forget or stop loving people just because they die, you know, Nick." His name now rolled off her lips naturally, which made her wonder if her first reaction to him was wearing thin. If she could just react to him like he was any normal man she didn't care about, then she'd be right on track. "They were married a long time. She has his two children."

"I understand that. It's just that she seems to have a number of related hang-ups. One big one is that she hasn't left the island since Larry died."

Rayne had to admit that at first she'd dismissed Tanya's problems and hoped they'd go away. However, lately, she'd begun to feel the same way as Nick. It definitely wasn't healthy to be so self-absorbed and trapped. "I've tried to persuade her to join me on a short trip in the hotel motor launch but she won't come. Sean's also tried."

"Then the family is aware that it's serious?"

"Yes, we're aware, although it's just Sean and me who know."

"And me, now."

Rayne nodded. It was strange that Tanya had let Nick know about her anxiety when they'd all gone to such great lengths to hide it from their own immediate family. She hoped it wasn't because Tanya trusted Nick, or was falling for him, especially after him telling her that he wasn't interested in her that way. She saw that Nick was expecting a comment from her. "Well, could be that telling someone else outside the family circle is easier. It's certainly a step in the right direction. I mean, it's up to Tanya to help herself, isn't it?"

Nick shifted his position slightly but remained hunkered down. "Absolutely. But a little shove in the right direction could also help."

"I've tried, believe me. Although she was better tonight than I've seen her be for a long time."

"Maybe it was having different company. We'll have to arrange more get-togethers."

Nick made it sound as if he were going to attach himself to them for the rest of his vacation. Feeling suffocated by him, Rayne slid off the rock and stood up, smoothing her skirt.

Nick also stood up and walked around the rock until he was beside her. "How did your brother come to be here in the first place?"

Rayne saw an opportunity to blow the Sinclair family horn and let Nick know once and for all that the island was theirs—forever. "Oh, he was sick and tired of his job in the automotive business. It was very routine, and, as you know, not very stable. He lived under the threat of layoffs. His first love was always sailing, which he did a great deal of on Lake Michigan, and eventually down here in the Caribbean. When my grandmother died, she left us all a little trust fund. The money gave Larry the means to purchase the resort."

"He died young, didn't he?"

"He had some kind of rare blood disease."

"That's really too bad."

Rayne wondered if Nick truly felt sympathy or was inwardly rejoicing that Larry was gone, leaving Tanya and Rayne as easy marks. The fact that

Nick had been here before indicated that he might have approached Larry about a sale in the past. There might possibly be something in the files that could give her more of a perspective on Lewis.

Nick eyed her. "Does Tanya help with the resort?"

"Sometimes when she's feeling up to it she handles the reception of the guests. Sean works around the resort as well. It's a family business. Everyone pulls their weight."

"But you pull the most, don't you?"

"I suppose I do." Rayne tossed her head and her bright hair cascaded over her shoulders. She thrust her hands into her skirt pockets. She wished he would just come right out and say what he wanted so she could turn him down and be done with it. She could be the one to bring up the subject, she supposed, but then why should she, when she had no inclination to deal with him? Why tempt fate?

"What did you do before you came here?"

"You mean, where did I work?"

"Yes. That's what I mean."

Excellent. Rayne had the chance to let him know who and what he was dealing with. "When I left college, I went to work for a corporation. I made it up to an administrative manager of a department, a department which they eliminated when they did some cost-cutting.''

Nick raised an eyebrow. ''A lot of people can tell the same story these days. But you must have been extra smart to have risen so quickly, so young.''

''I knew what I wanted and applied for the position when the other manager left to have a baby. I was surprised when I was accepted, but made the most of the experience. I had hoped to go higher. Anyway, my job disintegration coincided with Larry's illness and death, so I had a ready-made position here on the island.''

''No hassle being isolated in the B.V.I?''

''No. I don't find it isolated in the least.''

''Then you don't share the same problems as your sister-in-law?''

''No way. I enjoy traveling.'' Rayne dug her hands deeper into her pockets. Here was a chance to bait him. ''You must enjoy traveling as well.''

''I love traveling, but I also like staying put sometimes. A month's vacation on Silver Island will be more than a pleasure.''

Not for me, Rayne thought. ''So where do you live?''

''I have an apartment in Manhattan and a family place in Maine—a sort of escape hatch.''

And resorts all over the Caribbean, Rayne added silently. *Don't forget those, Mr. Lewis of*

Lewis Recreational Enterprises. Most men would have proudly mentioned their occupation, especially if they owned their own company. His deletion pinpointed Nick as being here for dubious reasons. "Sort of like a president might have?" she said aloud.

He grinned. "Yeah, sort of, but not on such a grand scale."

Except your presidency is of a resort management company. Come on, Lewis, ask me to sell Silver Island and get my answer, then you can leave tomorrow on the first transportation out.

But Nick didn't ask. He just stood close to her, his hands in his pockets, mirroring her pose. And all Rayne could hear above the lap of the sea was their breathing, and feel a sensation that she was slipping out of her real existence.

Nick broke the spell.

"Well, I think I'll make this an early night. It's been a pleasure meeting you, Rayne. See you around."

Nick's stride was much too brisk for the warm evening, and his departure was so abrupt that Rayne felt left in limbo, filled with a longing for something intangible.

Keeping her hands plunged into her pockets, Rayne continued her walk up the beach, deciding she had made all the wrong moves this evening. After dinner she should have returned to her villa and put a chair up to the door in lieu of a lock. She should have gone to bed and huddled under the sheet—it was too warm for the comforter. Better yet, she should not even have left her villa tonight. Dinner could have been delivered. Tanya could have been put off until tomorrow. If she'd done all those things, she wouldn't have met Nick Lewis. One consolation, she supposed, was that he hadn't mentioned anything about her spying on him, so, probably, he never saw her. That was a great relief.

Chapter Two

Wearing a black swimsuit, Rayne dangled her legs over the wall of rock edging the saltwater beach pool. Her swim was the third leg of her morning ritual. She began by lifting weights in her villa, followed by a jog along the beach. She always enjoyed herself thoroughly, feeling that she was in heaven; a heaven that she understood had been created by her brother's initiative in choosing Silver Island for his business venture in the first place. The circumstances of her takeover weren't to her liking, but at least Larry would be pleased that his young sister could enjoy the tranquillity of his tropical paradise.

Only this morning, Rayne was also aware that if she hadn't met Nick Lewis yesterday, she would have felt more tranquil. Instead, her nerves felt a prickling sensitivity to every little aggravation. Suddenly her world wasn't quite so complete.

Hoping to alleviate the discomfort with more exercise, she slipped into the cool water and struck out with a strong crawl. When she stopped for air and to tread water, she saw Nick at the edge of the pool, tugging a white T-shirt over his head. His black briefs magnified his athletic body. Wearing less clothing, he was even more overpowering. He waved.

Rayne returned his greeting with a brief salute. After all, he was a guest, and it was her duty to be cordial to him. She was sure he had a lot of friends in the hotel business that might make it a simple campaign to smear their resort with a few innuendos. Rayne had discovered early on that public relations was everything in the hotel business.

Nick dove in cleanly, swam toward her, and surfaced, wiping the moisture from his face with his hand. ''Morning, Rayne.''

His smile made his teeth flash white in the sun, in a way that wasn't at all reassuring. The type of smile one of his mother's dangerous heroes might possess. Trying to keep herself upbeat, Rayne said cheerily, ''Good morning, Nick.''

"This is a great pool hewn out of the rocks on the beach."

"Yes, isn't it?" Rayne felt like laughing and she wasn't sure why. It could possibly be that, at this moment, with Nick beside her, she felt cohesive once more. A line she was sure she'd read in one of C. T.'s books when the hero reappeared in the heroine's life.

Nick's eyes reflected the blue of the sky. "Was this pool here when your brother purchased the island?"

"Yes. But it was crumbling and looked a bit like a Mayan ruin. Larry had it fixed."

"So you have a freshwater pool up by the hotel and a saltwater pool down here. Excellent."

Rayne was thinking that this praise might be a lead-in for him to approach her about a purchase. She tensed, waiting, with negative answers ready to swarm forth.

But all he did was grin. "See you, then. Have a good day." Nick swam away.

Constantly conscious of Nick, Rayne finished her swim and heaved herself out onto the sea wall. She picked up her towel, wrapped it around her, and, without a backward glance at the pool, walked up the beach to her villa to change into her dress for work.

* * *

The marble floor of the hotel foyer was dotted with a myriad of plants in huge clay pots. Because of the open doors and roof skylights, everywhere was airy and bright.

Rayne's office was opposite the hotel reception desk. An ebony-skinned woman with upswept hair and a petite figure in a yellow sundress kept guard at a desk outside Rayne's door.

''Morning, Rayne,'' Rosie Baxter greeted her with a cheerful West Indian lilt. ''How was your Christmas?''

''Fabulous.'' Rayne smiled. ''How was yours?''

''Good. Juan gave me this.'' Rosie extended her left hand to display a cluster of sparkling diamonds.

Rayne admired the ring. ''Congratulations, Rosie.''

''We're ecstatic.''

''I should think. That's a wonderful Christmas present. When's the wedding?''

''We haven't actually planned anything definite yet, but you'll be invited.''

''I'll look forward to it. How's it been, Rosie? Busy?''

Rosie followed Rayne into her office with some file folders. ''Not too bad.''

Rayne loved her office. The pastel decor encouraged natural light to bounce from the many windows, and a ceiling fan purred above. French doors could be flung open onto a patio with a rattan table and matching armchairs padded with cushions.

Rosie placed the stuffed folders on Rayne's desk. "This is your mail since you've been away, Rayne. I dealt with everything that was urgent. Have you met Nick Lewis yet?"

The question surprised Rayne. Although it shouldn't have, she supposed. Wasn't it Rosie who was spreading the gossip? "Yes, I have."

"Did he say anything?"

Rayne sat down behind her desk to make herself feel more in charge. "Say anything about what, Rosie." *Play it dumb, Rayne.*

Rosie stroked her hands nervously down her skirt. "He owns a hotel management chain of his own. Don't you think it's strange he's here?"

"Lots of people like to vacation here, Rosie."

"I realize that."

Rayne steepled her hands. "Look, Rosie. I know what you're thinking. And I'm thinking it as well, but until he approaches me, everything is hearsay. And even if he does approach me, my answer will be negative. So you don't have to worry about your position here, because I know you do, what with your upcoming marriage and all."

"Thank you, Rayne. I know that Mrs. Sinclair

wouldn't sell either, but things being as they are . . .''

''Everything's just fine. The world's been going through a rough time economically, so people haven't got quite so much money to spend, but we're doing okay. We have our heads above water. We're not drowning yet.''

Rosie laughed. ''No. I know that. It's just . . . well I noticed that he had dinner with Mrs. Sinclair the night before you arrived home.''

''I know. I believe they've met before in the past.''

''Nick Lewis is a lot younger than Mrs. Sinclair,'' Rosie blurted out.

Rayne nodded. ''Nick's aware of that. It's only a friendship.'' The conversation reminded Rayne that she had to buy her sister-in-law a birthday gift for Sunday. ''Anyway, I think we're jumping our guns here, Rosie. Everything will be okay. Trust me.''

''Oh, I do trust you. I was just worried, that's all.''

''You've no reason to worry.''

''Good . . .'' Rosie seemed about to add more and Rayne thought she might have if she hadn't remembered propriety, something Rosie rarely thought about. But Rayne didn't mind. Rosie was a good worker with a quick mind. Her laid-back personality was exactly what Rayne needed to complement her own more high-strung fussy habits.

Rayne smiled. ''Rosie, don't you have work to do?''

''Unfortunately, I do. And so do you.'' After a frisky glance at Rayne's overloaded desk, Rosie left the office.

Rayne frowned at her desk, which was piled high with work. For once she wasn't too enthusiastic about attacking it. *That was the trouble with vacations,* she thought, *you wound down and got into the habit of doing nothing in particular. And there wasn't a better place in the world to do nothing in particular than Silver Island.*

Reluctantly Rayne tugged one of the file folders up in front of her, opened it, and picked up a pen. The pen reflected the uncommercial flavor of the islands in an office that as yet had shunned computers. Rayne always felt that if she could live without a TV, then she could live without a computer. Larry had often joked that they were lucky to even have telephones.

If a letter had to be typed, it was done so on the old black typewriter that delighted guests. Tanya or Sean wrote up the reservations in a big book. And all in all, they ran a smooth operation. An operation Nick Lewis would likely balk at. She could just see what would happen to Silver

Island if L.R.E. took over. The hum of technology would replace the hum of nature.

"You know," a male voice drawled from the door, "you do have an unusual first name."

Rayne looked up from the letter she was reading, or at least was trying to read. Nick's lean frame was now covered by white slacks and a black short-sleeved shirt. His light brown hair was damp and darkened from his swim and most likely a refreshing shower, and his eyes were bright and astute. Janet was right about not being able to avoid him. He kept popping up all over the place.

"I was a late-in-life baby and my parents were all set on having another boy," she explained. "They were going to call him Raymond, which is my father's second name. When I arrived they invented something quick."

"Do you push yourself beyond the limits because you weren't that boy they wanted?"

"How do you know I do?"

"It's obvious from what you told me about your quick rise in the corporation. Is that the reason?"

It really wasn't any of his business, but it was the truth. She'd always desired perfection and beat herself up over anything less. "Possibly having two older brothers also made me feel that I had something to prove."

''You were quite a bit younger than them?''

Rayne nodded. ''Yes. By the time I came along my father was used to the boys. I got left out if I didn't act like them.''

''I doubt if that's really true.''

''I'm not so sure about that. He never took me places, but he was always at ball games with the boys.''

''I wouldn't have minded a father who took me to ball games.''

Rayne remembered that his parents were divorced. ''I guess we all have our crosses to bear.''

His grin was lopsided, attractive, devastating. ''I guess we do. And you can ponder yours for the rest of the day while you're almost falling asleep over your work.''

Rayne put down her pen. ''Vacations play havoc with my concentration.''

''Ah, you are human.''

''What do you mean by that?''

Nick came to stand by her desk. He picked up the glass ball with the fake snow inside that the kids gave Rayne a Christmas ago.

''I thought maybe you were one of those robots that likely replaced your brother in the automotive factory.'' Nick shook the ball and stared at the miniature scene of children frolicking in the snow before replacing the glass ball on her desk.

"No, of course I'm not." Rayne squared her shoulders in defense because she hated confessing to any imperfections in her personality. And why was he here initiating this self-analysis anyway? "By the way, did you have something to ask me, or are you just passing time because you feel like playing psychiatrist for the morning? Come on, Nick, lay your cards on the table so everyone on Silver Island can get back to normal. Especially me."

Nick chuckled. "Passing by, and interested, actually that your office is run sans technology. Having come through the corporation scene, I would have expected you to be a technology freak."

Rayne pushed her hand through her hair. "I'm fully computer literate, but that's not the point here. Silver Island is what it is because of . . ."

"What it is," Nick finished, grinning.

"That's right. And it's not going to change for the time being."

"Don't get snappy. I'm here because it's natural. I wouldn't want it changed."

Oh, yeah, Rayne thought.

Nick plunged his hands into his pockets. "Anyhow, I'll let you be. See you later."

Hearing his footsteps recede, Rayne pushed aside her work. What was all that about? What she needed to do was what she had planned, and that was to look through the old files and check up on Mr. Nick Lewis. Then she might find out what he was all about.

She was down on her hands and knees rummaging through reams of ancient correspondence when Rosie came to the door. ''Rayne?''

Rayne glanced up. ''Yes, Rosie.''

''Rayne, I want to ask a favor. Juan's just called me and invited me to dine with his parents tonight in Spanish Town. It's Thursday and I usually go over to Tortola with the banking at noon. If I go to Tortola first I won't be back in time to get ready for Juan to pick me up, so . . . could I go to Road Town tomorrow morning instead?''

''Not really, Rosie. The banking should be done today. It always is. There are bills depending on the money being in the account. You'll be back in time, surely.''

''Not really . . . I . . .''

''Look,'' Rayne immediately had the idea that would take her out of the office but wouldn't make her feel that she had spent a totally worthless day. And she would also have a chance to buy Tanya a birthday present. ''Why don't I take the banking today? I'm not involved in anything here.'' She closed the file she had been looking in, as there was no letter in it from Nick's company.

"Oh, Rayne, thank you. I'll pay you back. I'll work extra hours. Anything."

"It's okay. I wouldn't mind a boat ride to clear my head."

"You're a dear."

"Think nothing of it. Run along."

Once Rayne had talked herself into her trip to Road Town, she grew excited about the prospect and hurried back to her villa to change into a willow-green dress splashed with golden sunflowers. She walked to the marina carrying a wide-brimmed straw hat with a ribbon around the crown that matched her dress. Yes, this was much better than being in the office, however delightful the office atmosphere was. She just didn't feel like reading letters and calculating figures today.

Rayne's step faltered and she crushed the straw hat between her fingers when she saw Nick waiting on the dock. Couldn't he get the message and leave her alone? Of course, Nick had no idea she was planning on going over to Road Town this afternoon. This was an unintentional meeting.

They couldn't ignore one another on the narrow dock beside the boat slip. Nick said, "Hi, Rayne."

"Hi. What are you doing here?"

"I'm staying at Silver Island on vacation, unless you've forgotten, and this afternoon I'm going over to Road Town for the afternoon. What about you? I thought you were settled in for a full day's work.''

''No. I'm taking Rosie's place and doing the banking. She has an important date with her new in-laws-to-be this evening and doesn't want to be late. She's engaged to be married.''

''That's nice. Therefore you grabbed the chance to leave the office, didn't you?'' He grinned.

Rayne nodded. She couldn't lie about her mood, which had been so obvious this morning. ''I'll get caught up on the weekend. Besides, this is also work.''

''But much more pleasant work. Don't you take the weekends off?''

''Usually. But not when I've just had a month off.''

''All work and no play, you know what they say.''

Rayne's auburn hair was caught by the saucy sea breeze. She stroked strands back from her forehead. ''I know what they say, but this isn't exactly the same as working in a big city, or for someone else. Whatever I do benefits the Sinclair family. Us.'' She emphasized Sinclair and us.

''True. But still you can't handle it all. You know, you should give Tanya some duties. Small ones, at first, to draw her in. She's capable.''

''I'm not so sure about that. She met Larry in

high school and they got married after graduation. Then Tanya got pregnant right away. She believed in being home for the children and Larry earned a good wage.''

''You're underestimating her, Rayne. Give her some space. Give her an opportunity.''

''If she wants one, I suppose. Has she said anything to you?''

''She mentioned that you do it all and don't seem to need help. I took that to mean that she wouldn't mind giving you some help if you would take it. Pleasantly, without argument.''

Rayne ruffled the rim of her hat with her fingers. ''You know, Nick. You're butting in where you shouldn't. You're a guest here. Remember that.''

Luckily, she didn't have to hear Nick's answer, as the hotel motor launch, piloted by Troy Chandler, circled into the marina and eased into the slip. Dusky skinned with thick curls and a stunning smile, Troy had been Larry's good friend. He jumped out.

''Hi, Rayne. Have a good vacation?''

''Too good,'' she told him, taking his hand and letting him help her aboard the boat. ''I can't settle back to work.''

Nick followed her in. ''This is Nick Lewis, Troy. He's a guest.''

''So you keep saying,'' Nick whispered in her ear, before he shook hands with Troy.

''Pleased to meet you, Nick. Make yourselves comfortable.''

Rayne and Nick sat next to one another on the padded seat. Troy fired the engine and the launch sped from the marina. Troy drove the boat the way Sean drove the Suzuki. Fast but sure. Rayne trusted them both.

Sir Francis Drake Channel was swollen by an east wind that made the ride extra choppy. Rayne swayed in Nick's direction and he placed his arm around her shoulders to keep her in place. Their eyes met, making Rayne feel as if she were afloat in a full-fledged storm. ''You don't have to hold on to me,'' she told him, hearing her voice tremble. Or was it the wind that made it sound trembly?

Nick didn't release his arm. ''Yes, I do, otherwise you'll be falling all over the place.''

His touch made Rayne panic. She didn't want to feel attracted to him. She wanted to keep the upper hand when it came time to negotiate with him. ''I travel on this boat all the time, without your arm around me, and I don't fall. Please, Nick.''

His fingers patted her shoulder. ''You are pleasing Nick.''

''Oh, Nick.''

He squeezed her shoulder. "All I'm doing is adding support so you won't tumble overboard. You're so uptight, Rayne. It's as if your vacation didn't help a bit."

"It did help." *It's coming back to find you here that's not helping.* She gritted her teeth.

"Then lean into me, not into the wind, and you won't feel as if you're fighting all the time."

Oh, so persuasive! But it did feel wonderful to rest against the curve of Nick's strong arm. It made Rayne realize how independent she tried to be all the time.

Nick smiled at her. "See, it's fine if you don't struggle."

Too fine, Rayne thought. She liked the feel of his arm around her.

Nick didn't release his arm until they docked at Wickhams Cay.

"Rocky ride," Troy apologized. "When do you two want to return?"

Troy was presuming they were here as a couple. That notion could begin a round of gossip. "I've only got the banking and a bit of shopping to do, Troy. About an hour or so. We're not together."

"Make it four hours, Troy," Nick said. "I want to do some sight-seeing, and we might as well go back together. Save you an extra trip."

"Fine with me. See you in four hours, right here."

Nick smiled. "Thanks, Troy."

Troy went to refuel the boat, leaving them alone, surrounded by an expansive view of the mountains and the sailboats in the harbor. The sun shone warmly on them.

To protect herself from the rays, Rayne put on her straw hat and tucked the strap of the matching bag over her shoulder. "You know, you do take a lot for granted. How do you know I'm not meeting someone here . . . for a liaison?"

Nick, hands in the pockets of his crisp white slacks, began to walk beside her. "Are you?"

"No," she said irritably. "But if I was, then you would be out of line."

"How do you know *I'm* not meeting someone here . . . for a liaison?

"You wouldn't want to be with me if you were, would you?"

"I might want to introduce you."

"Well, I'm not in the mood to meet anyone."

"Great. Because there isn't anyone. And you're not meeting anyone either. So we're squared."

The breeze threatened her hat and Rayne clamped her hand on the crown. "But I planned on being alone."

He chuckled. "Tough."

Road Town was clustered into two streets. The highway and Main Street. Traffic buzzed by on the left-hand side of the highway.

Rayne made to leave Nick by crossing the road. "I have to go to the bank now, so if you'll excuse me, I'll see you later."

"I'll wait."

"Surely you have something to do this afternoon, otherwise you wouldn't have taken the trip over."

He withdrew his hands from his pockets and gently touched her elbow to guide her across the road. "Nothing but sight-seeing."

His touch agitated her. She wanted it, yet she didn't. "Then don't let me stop you from sight-seeing."

"You're not stopping me. We have four hours."

They reached the opposite side and Rayne began walking toward the building that housed her bank. "Four hours that you set up, I might remind you."

"I'll admit to that."

"I'm pleased. You do realize that this is all your doing. Look, Nick, you might be on vacation, but I'm not. I'm not here this afternoon to sightsee."

"Why not? Business will be over as soon as

you walk out of the bank. What were you planning on doing after the bank for four hours?''

''I didn't plan on four hours. All I was going to do was get the banking done and shop for a birthday gift for Tanya.''

''When's her birthday?''

''Sunday. She's forty-three.''

''She doesn't look it.''

''No. She doesn't look it.'' Rayne saw that Nick's brilliant eyes were twinkling. He was amused while her emotions felt like a tumultuous sea.

''Look, Rayne, I really do think that you should return to work gradually, with less of a bump. I mean, you were trying to get everything cleared up in one morning.''

''No, I wasn't.''

''Yes, you were. I could see you were. Your desk was a mess and you hated it being that way. Everything you had to do was stressing you out.''

How did he know that? Rayne reached for the door handle of the bank. ''It's not true.''

''It is true. I'm like that myself. That's why I take long vacations. I've learned that I'd be a basket case if I kept going.''

''I just had a vacation.''

Nick grasped the door handle near her fingers. ''Yes, but you obviously didn't relax. I bet all

Christmas you were worried about the island, and how it might sink into the sea without you.''

Rayne bowed her head slightly. He had her right on.

His hand covered hers. ''It's true, isn't it?''

She relished the warmth of his large hand and nodded.

''So let's kick back a little this afternoon. These islands have a magic about them that makes romance irresistible. So, why not us?''

Whoops. Rayne hadn't been ready for that advance. Nick Lewis sure knew how to prod at people's vulnerabilities and when they wore down he knew exactly when to lower the boom. ''Not us, no.'' Panic edged Rayne's voice. She hoped he couldn't hear it.

His mouth curved attractively, reminding her of how comfortable his arm had been around her in the boat, while at the same time she felt uncomfortable and tense with him all the time. She was breathing heavily, wondering what he was going to come out with next. His hand snuggled upon hers.

''I can't believe you're unmoved by the beauty of the islands.''

Rayne's hat lifted in the gusty breeze. Nick adjusted it back on her head. Rayne touched his arm to support herself, then wished she hadn't. The warmth of his skin covered in crinkly hairs sent tingly vibrations through her fingers. At least his hand wasn't covering hers anymore. ''This conversation isn't about the beauty of the islands. It's about what I don't want, and that is a romance. Look, Nick, why don't we just meet back at the marina in four hours? Maybe you'll meet a lady to have a romance with. Go. Have fun.''

''I am having fun. I'll wait. And I can't understand why you wouldn't want a romance. You're a lovely woman.''

''It's with you I don't want a romance,'' Rayne said, then, feeling churned up inside, she left him outside the bank in the bright sunshine and went into the dimmer, cooler interior of the small building. No man would hang around after being told no so bluntly, she thought.

Rather than do banking business, Rayne felt like sitting in a cool place and collecting herself, but she immediately met Mr. Stinson, the manager, whom she usually dealt with, and he counted her deposits and checked Rosie's accounting.

''Things not that good at the resort, then?'' Mr. Stinson asked.

''Things are fine. Why?''

''Your credits are dwindling. Your debits are piling up. The new roofs for the villas and the air-conditioning in the hotel rooms last September were big expenditures.''

The air-conditioning had been Tanya's idea for

upgrading the hotel. The roofs had been leaking and were due to be done. "Our guest list is pretty full. We'll make it up. It's just a temporary situation."

"That's exactly what your brother used to say. For a start, I suggest that Mrs. Sinclair cut back on her personal expenses. That would help your cash flow a great deal."

"I don't want to have to do that."

Mr. Stinson wriggled his half-glasses on his nose. "You might need to, Rayne. You should talk to her."

Rayne never discussed the hotel finances with Tanya, as she didn't want to add to her sister-in-law's anxiety. "I can't."

Mr. Stinson laughed. "Didn't your mother ever tell you that there's no such word as *can't*? Look, Rayne, I advise you to talk to her—gently. She orders all her clothes from New York—expensive items, very expensive. If my wife bought clothes at those prices, we'd be bankrupt."

Rayne didn't want to divulge Tanya's problem, that she couldn't shop locally because she couldn't travel. Always a lover of clothes, Tanya mail-ordered her needs. "I know she has expensive tastes. I'll try and talk to her."

"If possible, do so. Thank you." Then Mr. Stinson cleared his throat. "Now, I understand that you have an offer from a hotel management company.''

''No, we haven't.'' And that was the truth. Nick hadn't approached her yet. But he'd obviously let the bank know his intentions. That move made her angry. Very angry. Janet was right. He was only here to propose business. And to think that she'd sat close to him on the boat and actually enjoyed his touch. And all that nonsense about romance with her. Just another way to get her on his side. Agitate her to a screaming pitch where she flung the island ownership at him. What a creep.

''I understood you might have had an offer by now. Anyway, if, and when you do, give the proposal some serious consideration.''

She was getting more and more angry at Nick. ''There's nothing to consider, Mr. Stinson. We're not receptive to buyouts.''

Mr. Stinson smiled slightly. ''You are definitely just like your brother. Stubborn. When you do get the offer, Rayne, give it some thought. That's all I'm saying.''

To appease the man, she told Mr. Stinson she would.

Feeling even more shaken after her meeting with Mr. Stinson, Rayne returned outside to the sunshine, hoping that Nick had given up and gone sight-seeing. Because she certainly wasn't receptive to Nick Lewis at this very moment.

Chapter Three

Nick was leaning against the blue-painted wall of a nearby crafts boutique, watching for her. Rayne ignored him and put on her hat and straightened her purse. Then she began walking.

He caught up with her.

"All go well?" he asked casually.

Not wanting him to see that she was disturbed, Rayne tried to bury her anger, wishing she wore dark glasses like he did. "All went very well." She heard a sharpness edge her tone.

"Then what shall we do now? Have a drink? I'm parched."

"You do that if you want. I plan to do my shopping."

"We can shop on our way to the restaurant."

"I don't want to be rushed."

"You won't be rushed. I'm cool."

Yeah, but I'm not, Rayne thought as she began to browse along a row of small boutiques. Maybe he would get bored with her shopping and that would give him the impetus to leave her alone. She walked into a clothes shop.

Nick followed her in.

Rayne went first to the rack of dresses. Slowly, she pushed one aside, felt the material between her fingertips, looked at the style and length, checked the size and the price tag.

"That's nice," Nick said. "But it's more for you. You look good in those slim, button-through affairs. Those flouncy sundresses suit Tanya."

Rayne didn't look at him. "I know what she looks good in. I'm only just beginning my shopping."

"Is that for you, then?"

"No. It's not for me." She slipped the dress back onto the rack and flipped her way through the rest of the stock. Nothing would suit Tanya. Nick was right. The dresses were more Rayne's style. There were only two blouses in the store, and Rayne didn't care for them. She left the store.

It took a visit to a number of stores before she found an ivory silk blouse that she felt would look nice on Tanya.

"Ah, now that will suit her," Nick agreed.

"Round neck, little pleats, sort of fancy. Very nice."

Rayne purchased the blouse, along with a skirt of a similar pale color, a shell necklace, and dangling earrings. She took her time, dawdling over her decisions, making small talk with the salespeople. Yet Nick was still with her. He was either one of those rare men who enjoyed shopping, or he would suffer anything for a business deal.

Their next stop was an art shop, where there were many framed pen and ink drawings of the local scenery.

Nick held up a view of the islands. "Does Tanya like this type of thing?"

"She adores the local artists."

"I'm going to buy this for her then. We should all celebrate together, go to another island for dinner. That way I can treat you both. Seeing I can't do it on Silver Island."

"That's not necessary, Nick. Tanya wouldn't expect it. And there will be Sean, as well."

"Sean can come. The more the merrier."

"No, Nick. You've forgotten that Tanya won't leave Silver Island."

"Why not let her make that decision? Don't you think it would be nice for her to leave the island for a change? It'll do her good. I'll book at Fisherman John's on a tiny island near Pelican Island."

Fisherman John's was owned by singer John Barth who'd had one classic hit. Everyone who was anyone wanted to go there. "I'm really not sure, Nick," Rayne said, but she could hear her conviction faltering. She'd love to be treated to Fisherman John's. It wasn't a restaurant she herself could afford.

"She'll be fine. You can't baby her forever, Rayne. One day you might not be around to take care of her."

Yes I will, Rayne thought. *You're not going to get rid of me that easily.*

"Don't override her chance to think for herself, to maybe give herself some hope that she won't always be tied to Larry's memory. You know what I mentioned on the dock. Give her space."

Rayne knew Nick was right. She'd been protecting Tanya for the past two years. Had she been overprotective? Should she just walk up to Tanya and tell her what Mr. Stinson had said and let her deal with the reality of their plight? Ask for help, as Nick had suggested?

"I want you to at least ask her, Rayne. And Sean. See what they say. If they say no, then fine, it's off. But give them the choice."

"All right," she agreed.

"Meanwhile, I'm going to buy her this drawing."

He purchased the drawing, tucked the package beneath his arm, and they returned outside. ''Do you have everything now?'' he asked.

''Yes.''

''Then let's go get that drink before I keel over from dehydration.''

If Rayne hadn't been so thirsty herself, she would have once again suggested they meet back at the marina. Not that Nick would have taken her suggestion. He seemed glued to her side for the rest of the afternoon.

Also, by now, she felt exhausted from everything that had happened. Therefore, she went with him to an outdoor bar and restaurant, where they sat at a table beneath an umbrella and ordered fruit drinks.

When they were settled, and Rayne was beginning to feel calmer, Nick rested his bare arms on the table. ''The bank give you the gears?'' he queried.

Nick had removed his sunglasses, so Rayne was able to stare into his blue eyes with their innocent long lashes. Deceiving eyes? ''Whatever gave you that idea?''

''You came out of the bank looking like you'd just endured a storm.''

Rayne twisted her straw in her drink. ''Well, you made me mad before I went in, and then, oh, you know bank managers, they panic over nothing. We had some heavy-duty repairs last year, that's all. But we'll get by all right. We always have. Larry operated on more of a shoestring than we do, and he made it. It's not your worry, anyway.'' *And it never will be.*

Nick placed some money on the table beneath his glass. ''But you are worrying?''

''No. I'm not. We'll get by. We always have.''

Nick reached over and touched her shoulder. His fingers found the back of her head and he massaged it slightly. ''You try to be so strong, Rayne.''

''I am strong.'' But even as Rayne spoke the words, she felt like bursting into tears.

He soothingly rubbed her neck. ''Sure you are. I've got an idea to pass the time so that you can calm down. Let's rent a vehicle and go for a drive.''

''We don't have time for that, Nick.''

''Yes, we do. We can make time. Rayne, don't be so argumentative. Why not give your brain a rest for a while? Think with your emotions.''

Which would make it much easier to get to me, she thought. *Sure, Nick.* ''I'm a cerebral person.''

''Even cerebral people enjoy drives. I haven't driven on Tortola for years.''

''When were you here last?'' Would Nick admit he was here not long ago, talking to Mr. Stinson?

"I was here just before Christmas."

Rayne was surprised that he should be so forth-right about his last visit. "That wasn't long ago."

"I have friends here, but they drove me up to their place. I didn't drive myself."

He slipped out of that one easily, she thought. No mention of a visit to her bank. "Do you have a B.V.I. temporary driver's license?"

"I can buy one at the rental shop. Don't put obstacles in the way."

She couldn't think of another obstacle. And why not let him have his way? Tortola was an island full of spectacular views. "All right. But we have to watch the time. We can't keep Troy waiting."

"We have hours." Nick released his gentle hold on her neck, got up from his chair, and picked up the parcels. "Tortola is named for the turtle dove, and I do believe doves are supposed to represent peace. So let's have some."

Rayne kept up with Nick's long stride. "Don't you like a good argument?"

"We're not having an argument. We're nig-gling at one another. Besides, I prefer rational discussions. I lived with two people who quar-reled constantly the first few years of my life, and I've made sure I never get into the same habit."

"Well, at least you learned something from your parents' relationship."

"I learned a lot, Rayne, believe me. Now, smile."

She smiled.

"Nice. You're a different person when you smile."

They walked to a car rental shop, where they managed to rent an open Jeep. There was no trouble for Nick to obtain a temporary B.V.I. license. Outside, on the road, he tossed their things in the back and Rayne settled into the passenger seat, feeling a thrill course through her veins. She hadn't driven around Tortola for years, either. In fact, she rarely left Silver Island unless she was returning home to the States. But it wasn't only the prospect of the drive that was thrilling. It was having Nick beside her, just the two of them. Alone.

Rayne hated to admit how much he attracted her, but he did. As long as she kept her head, she'd be all right, she thought, as they set off along the southern coast, every view of interest, from the turrets of the old Dutch Fort Burt, to newly constructed vacation villas. And always to their left was the island-studded Sir Francis Drake Channel, tossed by a light breeze and dazzling to the eyes in the brilliant sun.

They passed restaurants and marinas along the mainly flat coastal road. But the terrain changed when they reached the northern shore. Immediately they were driving up and down steep hills. Lush green forests climbed mountainsides and the blue water, with silver beach linings, sparkled in every cove. Rayne noticed that Nick was a careful driver, especially when hazards presented themselves; two-and four-legged animals often needed more than one honk on the horn to be made aware they were about to be made mincemeat if they didn't move out of the way.

She loved it here, she thought. She never wanted to leave. Ever.

She glanced at her companion, the one man who had it in his power to snatch everything from her. Why was she with him so intimately, side by side in an open vehicle, looking like any young couple out for an afternoon's sight-seeing trip? Why didn't she see the danger in him when she gazed at his handsome features, his thick, sun-streaked hair ruffled by the sea breeze, his capable hands holding the steering wheel?

Nick stopped the Jeep on top of a hill with a view of a small mooring harbor down below. "What are you thinking?" he asked.

"That it's breathtaking. I love it. I never want to leave."

"If your brother hadn't died, do you think you would be here?"

"No. I'd probably be coming here for vacations, though. Which wouldn't be the same. Although I hate the thought that he had to die to enable me to live here.''

Nick placed his arm across the back of the seat, his fingertips hovering only a few inches from her. ''He might have enlisted your help, eventually.''

''Maybe. After the first time I came here, I think in the back of my mind, I hoped I could one day settle here.''

''Is that how you feel, settled?''

Rayne nodded.

Nick stroked her breeze-rippled hair with the back of his hand. His knuckles grazed the bare flesh of her shoulder.

Rayne stiffened. Was he going to kiss her? ''Don't, Nick.''

He chuckled. ''Don't what? I was about to ask you a question.''

''That's fine.''

''Good. Do you have a boyfriend?''

She hadn't expected that type of question. She could lie, of course, and get rid of him that way, but she said. ''No.''

''Well, that's one consolation.'' His fingers fluttered down her arm. ''At least I'm not infringing on anyone else's territory.''

Rayne glanced at him. ''I am not territory.''

''Calm down. You know what I mean.''

Rayne smiled. ''I could be trampling all over

some woman's territory this afternoon, now couldn't I?''

''You could be, but you're not.''

''Isn't that a relief?''

''Why are you being so sarcastic?''

Because she was trying not to fall for his romance tricks, and it wasn't easy. ''Why don't we walk?''

''Sure. Why don't we walk? We haven't walked at all this afternoon. We didn't spend almost an hour shopping.''

Rayne glanced at him. ''*Me* sarcastic?''

He grinned. ''Let's go for a walk.''

They walked along the grass of the high cliff. The trees were kapok and the air smelled of hibiscus. Out at sea, a yacht left behind a white trail in the bay below them. Curving around the edge of the blue water was a strip of sand. A woman with a small child waded at the edge of the water.

A rental car drew up and parked beside their Jeep. A couple jumped out and came over to them. ''Hi! Would you mind taking a video of us?''

The good-looking blond man, who reminded Rayne of Larry, handed Nick a video camera.

''Not at all,'' Nick said. ''If you don't mind an amateur.''

''Anything. We just want to be together in the same video. Where are you from?''

"I'm from New York."

"And your wife?"

Rayne couldn't be bothered to correct them for such a short acquaintance. "Michigan. Where are you from?"

"Chicago, Illinois," the wife said. "I guess we're all escaping the winter. We hear it's been bad this year."

Nick had the camera ready to shoot. Rayne noticed he'd said amateur, but he knew how to use it.

Nick waved his hand. "Now *do* something, you two."

Nick followed the couple around with the camera for about ten minutes.

"Thanks," the man said when Nick had finished. "That's great. Where are you staying?"

"Silver Island."

"Sounds romantic," his wife chipped in. "Is it far?"

"Across the bay. There's just one resort."

"A family place," Rayne told them.

"Sounds interesting. We're staying down along the south coast. Maybe we'll come over and visit some day. This is Paula and I'm Scott."

"Nick and Rayne."

They all shook hands.

Scott smiled. "Very pleased to meet you. It's been fun, and thanks again."

"Drive carefully on these steep roads," Paula said, and the two then returned to their car, reversed, and took off.

Feeling dazed after the brief encounter, Rayne returned her gaze to the view of the aqua bay. It had been taken for granted that Nick and Rayne were a couple, an actual married couple. Did they look that compatible together?

Nick stood behind her. "Well, wife, what did you think of that?"

Rayne turned to face him. "I don't look like your wife."

"No. You don't. Too uptight." He grinned. "A wife of mine would be relaxed. Loved."

"Then why aren't you married, if you're the perfect husband?"

He reached out to touch her shoulder. "Never found the right woman."

"I'm sure there are women clamoring to be your wife." Rayne knew she sounded sarcastic again.

Nick traced his fingers over her hair. "No one has ever proposed to me."

"Well, don't look at me." Rayne moved out of his range so that his hand dropped. "Come on, we'd better get going. We'll be late."

They returned to the vehicle. As they took off Rayne looked at her watch and saw that they were definitely going to be late. Why hadn't she watched the time?

She was in a state when they had to stop for goats on the road. ''This was not a bright idea, Lewis.''

''Turtle Dove's remember.'' His teeth flashed white in the sun as they waited for the goats to clear the narrow road. ''I can't quite fathom you, Rayne. You love it here. You live here. But you haven't learned how to relax here.''

''So you keep saying. I've just never been a very relaxed person.''

''You dwell on all that might happen, instead of what is happening.''

''I have to, Nick. I've been responsible . . .''

''I know you have. You've pulled the weight for your brother's family, but I'm going to try and let you off the hook a little, at least by getting Tanya back to normal.''

''It's not your problem.''

''I've made it my problem.''

As the goats straggled off the road, Rayne gazed ahead, thinking that all this was probably another of Nick's ploys. If she focused on the moment instead of the future, then she'd be unprepared when he finally popped the question. Oh, no, Nick.

The goats cleared off the road. The farmer with

them waved. Nick waved and smiled, put the Jeep into gear, and continued driving.

It was all right for him, Rayne thought. He didn't have Stinson, the old worrywart, as Larry used to call him, breathing down his neck about his finances. Nick ran a successful financial company, a company he could use to buy out small family businesses with the blink of an eye. One wrong move by Rayne and everything could come crashing down around her family's fragile necks.

She'd never been so relieved about anything as when they switchbacked down Joe's Hill into Road Town. Rayne impatiently waited for Nick to return the vehicle.

Nick came out, slipping his wallet into his back pocket. He carried the parcels and they hurried down to the marina. "It was fun this afternoon."

"It was kind of nice to take a drive," Rayne admitted. "But we took too long a drive. We're really late. We should have taken into account we might meet goats and people with video cameras."

"Troy will wait. He knows we're coming."

"I hope so."

They rushed down to the marina. But neither Troy nor his boat were there.

Rayne certainly didn't feel like spending much more time alone with Nick, but after they had fought the B.V.I. telephone system to call Silver Island, to discover that Troy had waited, but had decided to take his other guests back, she knew she didn't have much choice. Troy would be another hour.

"Does Troy work for you?" Nick asked as they did their waiting by browsing the harbor-front stalls.

"He's contract. It's his own boat and we go yearly on an average number of trips. There's a contingency for a few extra trips, but if he goes over, we pay him extra."

"Does he ever go over?"

"No. Never. He's honest. Probably the people he had waiting grew impatient, so he felt he'd better take them. I mean, I'm not a guest, so I wouldn't be so unforgiving as guests he had to keep waiting."

"True. But I'm a guest. Remember?"

"You were the one who made us late."

"No. The goats made us really late."

Rayne laughed. "Okay. Blame it on the goats."

"Ah, you're now taking this with humor. That's good. The afternoon off must have helped."

"I'm hysterical," Rayne told him, but she was still laughing. She had relaxed this afternoon.

Nick stopped by a T-shirt stall. "I could do with more shirts."

Rayne watched him purchase a few, all different colors, knowing they would fit his muscled chest like a glove. More items to use as ammunition against her.

"Do you want one?" He held out a pretty sky blue T-shirt.

"It'll be too big for me."

"I like women in oversized men's clothing."

"I'm not obligated to do what you like."

"Take it." He tucked the T-shirt into her package. "Didn't you ever wear your steady boyfriend's jacket in school?"

"No. I didn't have a steady boyfriend in school."

"Studying all the time, I suppose."

"You're right. Nick, don't you think it's time we returned to the marina? We don't want to miss Troy again."

"And I wouldn't want you to have a nervous breakdown, either."

Rayne thought he sounded fed up with her. Was she really overanxious about life? An overachiever was what Larry had once called her. Was that bad? Or should she learn to even her life out and be a little less uptight? Changing her perspective didn't mean that she couldn't keep on top of Nick's motives.

On the marina, Nick sat astride a weathered post to wait. Rayne couldn't help it; she paced up and down. Regardless of whether she should or should not relax, she still had a lot of problems to think about. Most of all was Mr. Stinson's comments, which she had conveniently forgotten for the last hour or so.

When she returned to Silver Island, she would go to her office and really have a conscientious look at the books. She'd find some cost-cutting methods to employ and the resort would be fine. Mr. Stinson had just given her the jitters. If Rosie had come this afternoon, Rayne wouldn't have met with him, and, consequently, she wouldn't be in this state. She also wouldn't have spent the afternoon with Nick.

She glanced at Nick, who was watching her pace, as if amused by her distress. Did he know what she was thinking? And was he enjoying her discomfort, hoping that eventually she would be more than willing to grab his offer that would bale them out of their financial difficulties?

She met his gaze and Nick indicated the sea with a nod of his head. Rayne was relieved to see Troy and the launch.

"Sorry about this," Troy said when he helped Rayne into the launch. "I hope you didn't have to wait long."

"It's okay," Nick said. "Our fault. We went for a drive and met some goats."

"I figured it was something like that."

Rayne made sure she sat opposite Nick on the ride back, and not beside him. She had to remember that he was her enemy, not her ally.

Chapter Four

Rayne pushed the final ledger across her desk away from herself and kneaded her forehead with tired fingers. The lamp burned hotly over her desk, and perspiration had broken out on her flesh, making the fresh shorts and T-shirt she had put on this evening feel sticky. It would be months, maybe even a number of years, before the resort was in a stable position. How had this happened?

Sighing, she reached to turn off the lamp, leaving her office in darkness. She closed her eyes, listening to the cool night wind rustling the trees, and the gentle lull of surf rumbling to shore. Nick Lewis knew what he was doing. She'd slaved to bring the resort up to par with some of the more prestigious holiday spots in the Caribbean and been less frugal than she should have been. She had presented Nick with the perfect unstable setup to move in.

Rayne pushed back her chair and stood up. She stretched her arms and legs, numb from sitting so long. Now she had to tell her sister-in-law, who had been so carefree earlier this evening when she had opened her belated Christmas gifts, to take it easy, that Larry's dream could possibly fade, that all their dreams were in jeopardy. And Nick Lewis's might be the willing hands they could fall into.

Tanya was clearing up the reception desk when Rayne walked into the hotel foyer. "Have you finished working now?" she asked.

Rayne nodded. "For tonight. There's a lot to catch up on."

"I know. Sometimes I think you shoulder too much of the burden."

Hadn't Nick said the same thing? It seemed as if Nick's presence in her life was making her face up to facts. Just what he wanted, of course.

"No. I'm fine. I like working; you know that." Rayne gave her sister-in-law a second glance. She seemed melancholy. "Are you okay?"

Tanya let out a sigh. "Yes, I'm fine, I suppose. I had another fight with Sean tonight. He doesn't want to go back to college, and that's final. I'm not even sure if Larry would have had much pull with him. Sean's very stubborn.''

Rayne didn't know what to say. There really wasn't the money to send Sean back to college now. "Well, it's his life, Tanya. If he wants to follow in his father's footsteps, then that's how it should be.''

"But Larry was always adamant about the boys' education. He let college slip himself and regretted it. At least until he bought the island. That gave him a career challenge.''

Rayne leaned her arms on the reception desk. "Exactly. Larry didn't go to college but he did end up getting what he wanted, doing what he wanted. That's the main thing. If the island is Sean's ambition, then let him at least work it out for himself. He's still young. He might change his mind next year.''

Tanya put her hands on her hips. "You're not on my side, Rayne.''

"I am, but I'm also on Sean's side.'' Oh, dear, Rayne didn't have the heart to tell Tanya the truth, that it was lack of money that was causing her to take her nephew's side so adamantly. "Don't worry, Tanny, it'll all work out.'' She meant that for herself as well as Tanya. "Have you got time for a drink?''

"Of course.''

Tanya and Rayne walked to the terrace. There

were a few guests dotted about. For once, Rayne didn't see Nick. They chose a quiet, out-of-the-way corner and ordered fruit punch.

Tanya glanced at Rayne. "Something's bothering you, Rayne. You've been edgy all evening. You hardly ate anything at dinner."

The waiter put their drinks on the table. Rayne stirred the punch with a straw. Tanya looked so pretty in a full white skirt and a tangerine top, too young to be celebrating her forty-third birthday on Sunday—which suddenly made her recall Nick again, and the fact that Nick wanted them to celebrate Tanya's birthday with him. Before they'd parted at the marina, he had reminded her to mention the outing to Tanya. "I wasn't hungry. I went over to Road Town this afternoon, in Rosie's place, to do the banking, and I feel like I was out for too long in the hot sun."

"I hope you wore a hat."

"Yes, but it was windy on the boat ride and it wouldn't stay on." She didn't feel like mentioning the road trip around Tortola and the way she'd let the breeze free her hair, and the feel of Nick's knuckles caressing . . .

Tanya nodded. "I know you went. Rosie told me. And I saw Troy earlier and he said you traveled over with Nick Lewis."

"Yes. He just happened to share the boat ride over with me."

Tanya laughed. "And back I hear. Besides, that wouldn't be much of a hardship. He's really a sweetie."

A real sweetie, Rayne thought, feeling as if she were keeping secrets. Or was it being overly protective? At least she could start giving Tanya help by extending Nick's invitation. "Nick was with me when I bought your birthday gift and he invited us—you, me, and Sean—to celebrate your birthday at Fisherman John's." She realized she found it almost a relief to hand over some of the burden to Nick. He'd honed in on her wavering stress threshold from the beginning.

"Oh, wouldn't that be nice?" Tanya said. "I'm dying to go to Fisherman John's. The view is supposed to be fantastic, and the food superb. And that gorgeous John Barth owns the place, and apparently he sometimes sings. I loved that song, *All My Love Is for You,* that was such a tremendous hit."

"A one-hit wonder," Rayne murmured.

"So what? He made it big with that one song, which likely gave him the capital for Fisherman John's."

Rayne nodded. "I suppose. Then you wouldn't mind the boat ride?"

Tanya tugged at a strand of her long hair, looking disappointed. "Oh, I didn't think of that."

Rayne felt sorry for her. Tanya's life was going

to be ruined if she didn't get her act together. Although she didn't particularly want to spend more time with Nick herself, she would suffer for Tanya. "Come on, Tanny. You can do it. Troy won't let you come to any harm, and we'll all be there. Nick, who's big and strong. Sean too."

"That's true," Tanya agreed. "And it's only across the channel. I used to go across the channel all the time with . . . Larry." Her voice faded. "I don't miss him quite as much anymore, Rayne, but it's difficult, still."

Rayne touched Tanya's slim hand where the gold and diamonds that Larry had given her sparkled beneath the colored lights. "I know. It's difficult for me as well. But I think I've kept you down in some ways. I haven't given you the chance to get on with your life. Nick pointed that out to me when I wasn't sure if you would accept his invitation or not."

Tanya clutched Rayne's fingers. "I couldn't have survived without you, Rayne. I would have had to sell the island and go home. And I couldn't face home, not without Larry. I mean, Flint is where we met, where we dated . . . where it all started."

"I know," Rayne said softly. "So what do you say we go Sunday? I'd like to eat at Fisherman John's as well, and we certainly can't afford it ourselves."

Tanya nodded. "Yes, I agree. The prices I saw were triple ours. I read that some famous people dine there." She hesitated for a second. "Tell Nick we'll go. I'll be fine on the boat. I'll treat it as a little trip to sort of test my nerve."

Rayne couldn't help the broad smile that came over her features. "Great." Nick Lewis might be bad news on one account, but he'd turned out to be good news on another. "I'll tell Nick in the morning that it's on."

"Before I lose my courage."

"You won't. You'll have a wonderful birthday. It'll be a new beginning."

Tanya smiled. "I sure hope so."

Rayne realized she hoped so as well. Nick was so right. She had shouldered too much of the responsibility. She was tired.

Rayne decided to tell Nick the following morning, at the pool, but he wasn't there. She swam alone. Afterwards, Rayne went along to her office to find that Rosie might have tidied the files on her desk, but the work still remained. All an afternoon in Road Town had done was prolong the chores.

She worked for a couple of hours, then put a call through to Nick's villa, but he wasn't there. She had to find him. She wanted to make sure all the plans were in place so Tanya couldn't back out.

Thinking that Nick must be somewhere on the grounds, Rayne handed the reins of the office to Rosie and left the hotel. There had been a heavy downfall of rain first thing this morning. By now though everything had dried up and was sparkling. The sun shone warmly on her skin through her slim-cut ivory linen dress. A button-through. Nick's choice for her. Had she subconsciously dressed for him today? Rayne hoped not, but she could feel his presence around her all the time. He was a magnetic personality. Not a man easily forgotten.

Rayne eventually found Nick at the tennis courts. He was playing a game with Sean. Rayne stood by the fence and watched Nick in his white cotton shorts and polo shirt. He was agile on the court, a strong, forceful player. Sean seemed to be enjoying having a man as a partner. Sometimes he played with Tanya, who wasn't a novice, but she didn't have the strength of serve Nick had. She wasn't as challenging for her son's own solid game.

Nick saw Rayne first and gave her a little wave with his racket. Rayne indicated that she was going to wait for them. Nick mouthed that he wouldn't be long. Then Sean saw her and winked at her.

Rayne chose an umbrella table not far from the court. She bought three sodas and lime and sat sipping her drink, watching Nick, wishing circumstances were different, and that he was just a regular guest who was paying attention to her.

Nick and Sean joined her. Puffed out from the exertion in the heat, Nick tossed his racket onto the table and rubbed perspiration from his face and hair with a glistening white towel. Sean held on to his racket.

Rayne pointed to the drinks. ''You both look as if you could do with a cold drink.''

''Thanks, Auntie.'' Sean picked up a tumbler and gulped down the drink. ''I have to pick up some guests. Great game, Nick.''

''It was fun, Sean. Thanks. See you later.''

''Drive the guests carefully,'' Rayne warned Sean, and he gave her a thumbs-up sign, which she took to mean that she was making headway with Nick romantically.

Nick slung the towel over the back of a chair. ''I sure could do with a drink. Thanks, Rayne. Very thoughtful.''

''It's club soda and lime.''

''Fine.'' Nick sat down and drank half the liquid in one gulp. ''I needed that. And I hope what you're going to tell me is positive because I went ahead and took the initiative to book up Fisherman John's. Being new, they're busy. Sean was all for it.''

Rayne sipped her own drink. Nick seemed to increase in size each time she saw him. Flushed from his exercise, he appeared all muscle. She couldn't take her eyes off his powerful forearms resting on the table. But she had to. She lifted her gaze to meet his questioning one.

''Yes, it's positive. Tanya really wants to go to Fisherman John's, and I think her desire will outweigh her anxiety.''

''What about you?'' he asked.

''What about me?''

''Do you want to go?''

''Naturally. There's been a lot of hype about the restaurant. I always like to see what other places are doing.''

''With an operation like this, it's essential for you to know.''

''Yes, that's very true.'' Rayne sensed an awkwardness, likely caused by a lot left unspoken. She finished her drink. ''I'll go and tell Tanya that everything is arranged. Then she can't back out.'' She stood up.

Nick also got to his feet and picked up his racket and towel. He slung the towel around his neck. ''Don't let her.''

''I won't. Thanks for the help.''

"I'll help anyone or anything that's not living up to potential."

Which also includes Silver Island, Rayne thought. She had to remember that business was still his real reason for being here. But it was difficult to remember anything much when she was standing with him, noting the way the warm sunshine highlighted the blond streaks in his hair and emphasized his vitality.

Nick's eyes were hot blue, searing . . . Rayne dropped her gaze. "I have to go."

He nodded. "See you later. I'll let you know the time."

"Thanks. Leave a message with Rosie if I'm not around."

"Or Tanya. She's capable."

"Yes, she is." Rayne smiled.

Nick returned her smile. "Bye. Thanks again for the drink."

One of them had to make the first move. Nick chose to walk away first. By this time, Rayne's heart was pounding so hard that her chest ached painfully.

When Rayne returned to the hotel, she didn't procrastinate about telling her sister-in-law that all the plans were made for Sunday.

"That sounds wonderful, Rayne. Sean is thrilled. Not only does he think Nick's cool, but he also thinks I should get a life and this is a start.''

''That's good. As long as you're okay about the boat trip.''

''Yes. Isn't that funny? I'm actually looking forward to it. I think I've been a little silly.''

''No, you haven't. A lot of people have anxiety trouble.''

''I hope that's true. You've always been fine.''

Only because she had never subjected herself to the level of intimacy with a man that Tanya had. She played it safe. No emotional involvement. No hurt. Until now. She knew already that Nick Lewis was carving a segment of himself into her brain, a piece of himself that might always be there.

Rayne found another piece of Nick on Saturday evening when she opened her parcels to wrap Tanya's gift. The soft blue T-shirt with a discreet B.V.I. inscription on the chest was amongst her purchases. First of all, she tossed it to one side while she neatly wrapped Tanya's gift. She wrote the card and put the present on her table.

Then she picked up the T-shirt again. It was the truth. She'd never worn a boyfriend's jacket, or anything having to do with a boyfriend. She'd never had many boyfriends.

Impulsively, she walked into her bedroom and

stood in front of the mirror. She unbuttoned her dress and slipped out of it. Then she pulled the T-shirt over her head. Although Nick had never worn the shirt, and even though she knew she was being foolish, she felt as if Nick were touching her.

She pulled on a pair of white shorts just as there came a rap at the door.

The door was open and Nick was standing there when she reached it. For once she wished there were locks. Big ones. Why did he have to arrive at the very moment she was parading around in his T-shirt?

"Hi." His eyes scanned her. "It looks great. That shade of blue suits you."

She fingered the T-shirt. "It's a bit big. You should really . . ."

"It's yours," he said firmly. "I don't take gifts back, once I've given them."

"I didn't ask for a gift in the first place."

"You didn't have to ask. I wanted to give. Now. Forget it. I've just come to check that everything's okay for tomorrow with Tanya."

"So far."

"Good. I talked to Troy and he's going to give us as smooth a ride as possible. And John Barth is expecting us."

"You know John?"

Nick nodded. ''I was staying somewhere once where John was the entertainment. We met.''

''He's retired from singing, though, isn't he?''

''Not entirely. He still likes to entertain.''

''I'm looking forward to it.''

''So am I. By the way, do you have another sheet of that wrapping paper that I can use for my gift to Tanya?''

''Yes. I have an entire package. I brought it with me from home.'' She walked into the kitchen, opened a cupboard, and took out a couple of sheets. Nick was right behind her. She handed him the paper. ''Is that enough? The picture's quite large.''

His fingers brushed hers as he took the paper. ''Yes, it's enough. Thanks. This is a big villa, isn't it?''

''Two bedrooms. Tanya wanted me to have enough room so I could invite friends or family to stay if I wanted.''

''But you don't, do you?'' Nick grinned. ''You keep work work working and slave slave slaving away. You'll end up with your brother one of these days. Six feet under, prematurely.''

''You're exaggerating, Nick.''

''Well, maybe a little, but I think you should cheer up and enjoy tomorrow evening, for Tanya.''

''I am going to enjoy myself. Don't fret.''

Rayne laughed. "Come on, Nick, I do think of more than work. However, my prime concern is my family, and my work happens to be the vehicle that keeps them fed and happy."

He rolled the sheets of gift wrap into a tube. "Yeah, I realize that. And I'm a fine one to talk. I've worked my butt off all my life."

Tell me how, Nick, Rayne thought. Out with it. Then she decided she didn't want to know at that moment. She wanted to celebrate Tanya's birthday in peace and not spoil the affair.

Nick saluted with the roll of paper. "See you tomorrow, then."

Rayne felt dispirited when he closed the door behind him.

On Sunday Tanya opened her gifts before they left for dinner. Everything she was given was admired and loved immediately. While everyone else appeared quite carefree, Rayne felt taut with apprehension. Tanya seemed fine at this very moment, but what if she got cold feet by the time they reached the marina? Tanya would be so embarrassed to make a fuss in front of Nick. This really wasn't a good idea.

The gifts were put away and Sean solicited one of the waiters to drive them down to the marina in the Suzuki. With Sean also in the back, Rayne was squeezed beside Nick, which didn't help her uneasiness. He put his arm around her shoulders to hold her into the vehicle, reminding her of their trip across the channel to Road Town. And the way they'd sat in the car on the hill overlooking the channel. And the goats that had delayed them . . . For some reason that outing had etched itself in Rayne's mind as being something wonderful that had happened to her. And yet, really, all they'd done was niggle at one another. She'd been so negative with him.

Well, she had a reason to be negative. He was here for entirely different reasons than the ones he was displaying. Everything he did was a lead-in to a finale that once again would meet Rayne's negativity.

Carl drove slower than Sean, and Rayne wondered if they were ever going to reach the marina. Nick's fingers beat a slow melodious tattoo on her shoulder bone. She turned to look at him and he bent slightly and brushed her hair with his lips. If he kept that up, how would she endure the evening? And in front of everyone, too.

As soon as the Suzuki stopped, Rayne quickly disentangled herself from Nick's arm and jumped out of the vehicle.

Nick landed beside her. "Are you frightened of me, or afraid Tanya's going to fall to pieces?"

"The latter," Rayne told him, as they moved along the marina, Rayne about a foot ahead of him, rushing. Of course she was afraid of him. If she did fall in love with him, when the time came for her to turn down his proposal, he would leave her. Flat. She had no doubt of that.

''Don't worry. I think she's going to be fine.''

And she was. Tanya seemed to forget she was even in a boat as they chatted and laughed on the way over. Before they knew it, they were docking at the small island.

Except for a one-story stucco hotel, Fisherman John's was the only other building on an island half the size of Silver Island. There was a wooden dock, which looked a little bedraggled beside the luxury seagoing vessels moored there. Troy pulled into a slip and they all disembarked, Nick and Sean showing concern for Tanya, who still seemed in good spirits.

''Isn't this wonderful?'' Tanya said. ''The restaurant's so quaint.''

And indeed it was, Rayne agreed. A short trek across a narrow silver beach there appeared to be a sprawling hut, with only a palm roof for cover; chairs and tables were scattered across a wooden floor. It was crowded. John Barth now drew his fans with succulent food, a trillion-dollar view, and various celebrities who sailed over to dine at the *in* place of the moment. Cajun cooking aromas wafted through the air.

Their table was in an airy location, overlooking

the sea. Rayne sat next to Nick. John Barth strolled over to talk to Nick, and to be introduced to Nick's guests. John, who was in his early forties, with salt-and-pepper hair and a twinkling smile, wished Tanya a happy birthday and promptly went to the microphone set up on the small entertainment stage.

"Let us all wish Tanya Sinclair from Silver Island a hearty happy birthday this evening," he said, and led the crowd to sing "Happy Birthday to You . . ."

Tanya flushed under the scrutiny. "Oh, dear, you shouldn't have said a word, Nick."

Nick patted her hand. "Enjoy. Don't be bashful."

Rayne glanced at her menu. Nick was being so good to Tanya, she hated to think that he might have an ulterior motive. She hadn't thought of it before, but what if this trip off the island was his way of showing Tanya that she was free to leave? In other words, a way to remove a barrier to his goal of acquiring Silver Island. Because all the time Tanya wouldn't budge, Nick was stymied. Could Tanya's problems be the reason he hadn't mentioned anything to Rayne as yet? He'd sure jumped at a chance to help her sister-in-law.

Rayne frowned. She hoped that Nick wasn't that mean. Tanya was having such a good time. But Tanya was also fragile. If she thought she was going to lose the island, she might withdraw into her shell.

Nick's gaze rested on her and he frowned at her expression. ''Something the matter?'' he asked softly.

She shook her head. She wasn't going to start anything. Not on Tanya's birthday. And, after all, the idea was only a supposition. Nick's motives might be completely altruistic. ''I'm having a great time.''

Nick smirked. ''Then look like it.''

''Why do you keep getting on me? Maybe this is my normal expression.''

''It's not. You're worrying about Tanya. Don't. She's old enough to look after herself. Worry about me, instead, if you insist on worrying about someone.''

''Why you?''

He leaned over slightly, his bare arm brushing hers. ''Because I like you and I don't think you like me.''

''That's not true. You're okay.''

''Thanks a lot.''

''I just don't want something that's not going to last. You're only here for a month.''

''You mean if I was going to live here, you might consider a romance with me?''

''Well, you're not going to live here, are you, so that's just hypothetical.''

"I could afford to live here."

I bet, Rayne thought, as a guitarist, singing island songs, serenaded them. "Let's listen to the music."

He sat back in his seat. "All right."

The guitarist continued the serenade all through the delicious meal, and at the dessert course a birthday cake was presented to Tanya.

Another of Nick's doings, Rayne thought, as Tanya made her wish and blew out the candles. He didn't miss a trick. She prayed that none of this was a trick.

After dinner, John returned to invite Tanya to dance, and a young woman in a short white dress shyly claimed Sean for a dance. Nick and Rayne glanced at one another as Sean accompanied her to the now-crowded floor.

"Do you want to dance, or do you want to escape and walk off our meal on the beach?" Nick asked.

Either was dangerous. Although walking was likely the lesser of the two intimacies. "I'll choose the walk."

They reached the beach, guitar strains filling the air and traveling with them. The musical notes skipped over waves that seemed to have more force than the sea surrounding Silver Island. Surf broke on the beach not far from their feet.

Nick took Rayne's hand to help her over some low rocks. "Careful. The sea is rougher here."

She was going to pull her hand away from his when she was safe, but he clasped her fingers firmly.

"Enjoying yourself?" he asked.

"Wonderful. Thanks, Nick. You thought of everything. And the change is obviously doing Tanya a world of good." And you'd better be on the up and up.

"Maybe she'll have a romance with John."

"Isn't he married?"

"He has been, twice. His last wife died in a car accident, so they'll have something in common."

"I don't know if Tanya's ready for a relationship."

"That's up to Tanya, isn't it?"

"Yes, it is."

He squeezed her fingers. "That's it. Let her go. Besides, Tanya deserves some fun. She did well on the boat. And she's too young to hide herself away. Larry wouldn't want her to, I'm sure."

"I know he wouldn't. He'd only want her to be happy."

"Then let her do what she wants."

"As long as she doesn't get hurt."

Nick stopped walking and they stood watching the dark sea that occasionally erupted with white caps. "If you fall in love, you take the risk of getting hurt. Whether it ends up someone leaves or dies."

"I realize that. Have you ever taken that risk?" She remembered he'd told her that he hadn't found the right woman.

"I'd have to be pretty sure I'd found the right person to take the risk with. Divorced kids always wonder if they'll end up the same way, so we shy away from anything too serious." Nick reached out to brush a stray strand of bright hair from her face. "How about you?"

His tender touch made Rayne tremble. She let out a deep breath. "No. I've never taken the risk."

"Then it's about time you did."

Nick lowered his head and covered her mouth with his. Immediately Rayne stiffened and Nick seemed as if he was about to draw away, but then, she couldn't help herself, her lips yielded and the gentle persuasion of, his kiss lulled her to move closer to him. She stroked her fingers through his thick hair and closed her eyes.

Tossed. Turned. Like in the midst of a storm. Rayne knew she should stop, but there was too much excitement in Nick's touch, too much promise. She gripped him tightly, until, at last, as if he couldn't kiss anymore, his mouth eased its pressure and they moved apart.

Nick reached out and touched Rayne's sleek hair. He stroked it over her shoulder. "I knew romance with you would be fun."

This wasn't fun. She was on the verge of doing something foolish with Nick Lewis, a man who had motives far beyond romance, a man who had the power to completely change her life. Destroy her life. And not only her life. Tanya's and Sean's as well.

Rayne moved far enough away so that his hand fell. "Don't you think we should go and see if Tanya and Sean are ready to leave? Troy will be here soon." She could barely speak. Her words sounded like little squeaks.

"Not for a while. Calm down first. I'm not sorry we kissed, Rayne."

No. *Because now you know how much you attract me.* She scrubbed back her hair with her hands and sighed.

"We've been leading up to it," he added softly. "It was inevitable."

"I agree," she said shakily. "But I don't think it should happen again. It's not what I want."

Nick pushed his hands into his slacks pockets. "You mean, you didn't like it?"

Rayne thought his words sounded stilted. Hurt? "No. I don't mean that. I just mean that, there's no time in my life for such . . . dalliances."

"There's not much time in my life either. But

I'd make time if necessary. If things worked out that way. Isn't that what love is all about? You're single and then you're double and your aims become double.''

''I've never really given it much thought, Nick.''

''Well, now you can. We've kissed, it was pretty nice. Therefore, we can think about being together more.''

''We can't be together more than we've already been.''

''Something was drawing us together.''

''You,'' Rayne said. ''You were the one who kept popping up all over the place, getting in my way. You suggested this thing for Tanya.''

''Which has worked out extremely well. So don't be mean.''

''I'm not being mean. I'm just saying that you initiated everything between us. You were at dinner my first night home. You came to my office. You were on the marina going over to Road Town. You were the one who made the four-hour arrangement. You were the one who suggested the drive and made us late.''

''Maybe it's because I like being with you. Ever thought of that?''

Rayne didn't have a chance to answer him. Nick strode away up the beach toward Tanya and Sean who were coming across the sand.

After taking a deep breath, Rayne rushed to join them. She smiled at Tanya. ''Hi. Had enough dancing?''

''Yes. I'm dead on my feet.''

Rayne fell into step beside her sister-in-law, leaving Nick and Sean to follow. ''All ready for the return trip?''

''Why not? I feel quite confident.''

''That's wonderful.'' If Nick had done nothing else, he'd helped Tanya. For that, Rayne would always be grateful.

Chapter Five

Rayne caught up on some work the following morning. For entire chunks of time she forgot about Nick and that the resort was in jeopardy. How could Silver Island really be in trouble when she always had so much work to do, and there were so many guests swarming around? What it came down to was that next season they would have no choice but to raise their rates. They'd kept them below par for far too long. She'd been trying to run a deluxe resort at economy prices. She would revise the rate schedule for next September.

Feeling relieved that she might have come across the solution to their dilemma, at lunchtime Rayne took a sandwich and a magazine down to the marina. There was a ridge of seawall where she liked to sit and watch the boats.

She had just finished her meal when she saw Nick leaving a blue and white boat named *Bright Sail*. She followed his trek up the marina, admiring the way the sun glinted on his hair, making it appear as if it had golden streaks. As usual, his shorts and one of his white T-shirts emphasized his athletic build; and his dark glasses made him appear mysterious. To even give a casual thought to having been held in those strong arms and kissed made Rayne's heart pound like a sledgehammer.

Nick sat down beside her, bracing himself on the wall with his hands. ''Hi. Lunch hour for the working girl?''

Rayne made a face at him. ''There's a great deal of work. I can't be lying around sunning myself all day. Or playing Captain Bareboater on fancy yachts. Who does the boat belong to?''

Nick clapped one hand to his heart. ''Does she really want to know something absolutely frivolous like who the boat belongs to?''

Rayne began to laugh. ''Nick. Don't be so silly. Naturally I'm interested. Who does it belong to?''

''A guy I went to college with leaves it sit in the dock at his home on Tortola most of the time. He works more hours on Wall Street than I've had days in my life. Anyway, even though his parents live in the house, they don't use the boat. So he gave me carte blanche to use it.''

''Did you go over to Tortola to pick it up?''

''Your astuteness continues to amaze me.''

By this time Rayne was laughing hard. ''Do you know how to sail?''

He grinned. ''Basically. Do you?''

''I've never sailed anything that big.''

''There's a good strong motor, so you don't have to rely on the sails. Do you want a ride in it?''

Rayne glanced at the gleaming boat. ''I wouldn't mind. But it would have to be later.'' Danger signals flashed but she ignored them. Humor had obviously softened her.

''Later's fine.''

Unwise move, Rayne's brain screamed, but her mouth said, ''Great.''

''What time can you be off work?'' Nick asked.

''Three-thirty.''

''Terrific. You can meet me down here at four.''

''That's fine, but what about dinner?''

''I'll rustle up a snack. We'll anchor and eat aboard.''

''Excellent.''

Nick hoisted himself with his hands and landed

on his feet in front of her. He touched his finger briefly to the tip of her nose. ''See you on *Bright Sail* at four, then.''

Don't try and make sense of this, Rayne told herself, as she returned to the office. Just go with the flow.

Rayne left work early to shower and change into a white T-shirt, cream, shorts and deck shoes. She put on a baseball cap and dark glasses for sun protection. Nick was waiting on board also in shorts and his mulberry T-shirt.

Nick put out his hand when she reached him. ''Hi. I thought you'd forgotten.''

Rayne took his hand, noticing how his lean strong fingers curved around her own and squeezed tightly, almost as if he'd been anxious. ''I'm sorry I'm a little late. I got hung up with a phone call and I stopped to shower . . .''

''It's okay. Just so long as you did come. I've got a picnic for two in the fridge.''

So that's why he's worried, Rayne thought as he helped her aboard. He didn't want the picnic to go to waste. She released her hand from his quickly, reminding herself not to forget that all Nick's motives were suspect.

Rayne supposed that she shouldn't be surprised that Nick was a competent sailor when his appearance resembled that of an athlete.

"Are you going to help?" he asked, as they prepared to set sail.

"Sure. Just yell instructions."

Not having had experience on such a large boat, Rayne was amazed when they were actually up and sailing. Nick proposed to head around Silver Island and anchor on the south side. Rayne had been on that side of the island before. She loved it there. Calm aqua sea filled with colorful ocean life, and half-moon desert-island beaches ridged by bowing palms and a jungle of palmettos.

They anchored off one of the beaches and, in the neat little galley, shared the job of fixing the meal of chicken, pasta and fresh salad, crusty garlic bread, and a basket of juicy luscious fruit— the *honeymoon* picnic package the Bay View Terrace restaurant put together.

Why the honeymoon picnic?

Nick slid dishes containing their meal on to a tray. "Got a problem?"

"No." Rayne decided to keep cool. His choice of picnic might not mean anything, other than he preferred the choice of food. "Where are we eating?"

"On deck. You go up. I'll serve."

Rayne climbed the steps to the deck. Nick had already erected a table between two of the seating berths. She sat down on one side while he set out their meal. He put out a couple of cans of soda with glasses.

"It's not safe to drink and sail." He smiled.

Rayne agreed. She really liked Nick's thoughtfulness, his sensible nature.

They ate while the sun slipped away, turning blue sky to red, and the water from an aquamarine gem to black velvet. Rayne had to admit that the resort's *honeymoon* meal was a winner. Designed to lure the couple into a romantic mood.

And that gave her an idea. Honeymooners. Instead of just offering a mere honeymoon picnic at the bottom of the restaurant menu, why not aim more of their advertising dollars at romance? In September, when they raised their rates, they could couple the rate raise with a complete honeymoon package. It would lessen the blow and disguise the increase somewhat.

Oh, Nick, she thought, you won't get to me now. I've got my answer to save Silver Island from your clutches.

Content that she was in control, but also replete from the delicious meal and lulled by the gentle lap of waves against the boat, Rayne leaned her head against a cushion. "This was a wonderful idea, Nick." Great idea, Nick. You've unwittingly given me some positive ammunition.

Nick, resting his arms on the table, gave her an intent stare. "I'm pleased you think so. I had the feeling that you weren't overly impressed with the entire evening.''

Rayne heard the edge to his tone. ''When I showed up you seemed more worried about the food going to waste than me, that's why.'' It was part of the reason, anyway.

''I would have managed to eat it all.''

Rayne brushed a stray strand of hair from her cheek. ''Then it wasn't the food?''

''No, of course not. I wanted you to come with me this evening. You know that.''

''Do I?''

''You should. After last night on the beach at Fisherman John's. You know, Rayne, I spent so many years making plans with my parents, only to have them cancelled, that I don't believe anything is going to truly happen until it actually does. So when I saw you coming up the marina, I was relieved and I suppose it put me a little off balance when you actually came aboard.''

Rayne could tell that his admission came from his heart. ''Why did your parents do that to you?''

''I don't think they were conscious of doing it. Mostly their work interfered with their plans. Mother, especially, had to work extra hard. There were some lean years when she had very little to support us.''

''Didn't your father help her raise you?''

''She was too proud to take anything from him. For a long time I never saw him. When I was old enough to make up my own mind whether I could see my father or not, we met and got together. He'd had a struggle as well, but he gave me a little financial help to get my business off the ground. Guilt money.'' Nick grimaced.

''That's probably not true, Nick.''

''Probably not, but I felt that way at the time.''

The sky was darkening now and Rayne felt that they had been out long enough. So she raised herself from the berth and began to clear the table. ''We'd better do the dishes and tidy up the galley.''

Nick observed her frantic movements. ''What have I done now?''

Rayne piled one plate on top of another. ''Nothing. I have to work tomorrow. I can't be too late getting back.''

Nick rose and came around behind her. ''I wasn't intending to get back late. But I didn't intend for you to be a waitress either. I can clean up later or tomorrow morning. There's no hurry.'' He placed his fingers around each of her wrists and made her release the plates. ''Don't have a fit. I mean, it's not exactly as if you have a boss waiting to clock you in first thing in the morning.'' He caressed the slender bones of her wrists. ''I would have thought the island pace might have slowed you down by now. You're too tense about a type of work that should be a pleasure.''

Nick was so close to her that Rayne could feel the warmth of his body radiating into hers. If she as much as flinched she knew that their bare legs would brush.

''You've told me that before, Nick.''

''And I'll repeat it until you get the message.'' He seemed to reluctantly remove his fingers from her wrists. Then he moved away from her.

Rayne slid both hands agitatedly through her hair, and then turned around to look at Nick. He was standing by the boat rail, the golden hues of his hair illuminated by the moon. How easy to move through the small space between them, to throw back her head, to invite his mouth to crush hers . . . how easy to lose perspective.

''Do you want to leave right away?'' Nick asked.

''When we've cleaned up.''

''Then let's clean up before you lose a screw over it. We'll motor back.''

Rayne heard the same type of tone she'd heard when they were in Road Town. He was getting fed up with her. Well, what was she supposed to do? Make love with him? Become so vulnerable that she'd do anything he asked? In particular, release the island to L.R.E.?

No. She refused to fall for his manipulation.

They cleaned up and then Rayne followed Nick to the top deck so they could motor home. Realizing there was nothing she could do to help, she chose a seat in the stern and tucked her sunglasses into her baseball cap on her lap. A pleasant evening had turned slightly sour and she couldn't really pinpoint why. Well, she could. At all times, at the back of her mind, was Nick's *real* reason for being here and it put a damper on everything. It made all their actions together worthless.

Nick's bad language jerked Rayne from her thoughts. Obviously something was wrong. Then she realized what it was. The boat hadn't started moving. The motor wasn't turning over.

"We could use the sail," Rayne suggested.

Nick raised his hand into the air. "Feel it."

She nodded. "Calm. Well, we'll have to wait for a breeze to come up."

"You'll be back late."

"It can't be helped."

"But you were in such a rush a while ago."

"We can't help the engine, Nick."

"At least you're not panicking. It'll give me time to try and fix it."

They constructed a temporary lamp over the engine and found the toolbox. Rayne acted like a surgeon's assistant as Nick worked on the engine.

Nick picked grime from a spark plug. He blew away the grains of dirt. "I didn't think that because Rod never uses the boat that he wouldn't keep the maintenance up. The guy earns enough to pay a fleet of mechanics."

Rayne, sitting cross-legged on the deck next to Nick, laughed.

"This is not funny. This is the proverbial run-out-of-gas trick, except I packed an extra gas can."

"I'm not blaming you, Nick. Really. Would you like me to make some coffee?"

"Yes, please. You've been a great help. You knew what tool to hand me at the very precise time I needed it."

The compliment warmed her. "I had brothers, remember?"

"You did this for them?"

"All the time. It was the only way I could get their attention when they worked on their cars."

"You really did feel left out, didn't you? What about your mother?"

"She's great, but likes to do a lot of volunteer work and help others."

"But not her family?"

"Oh, yes. I'm not saying they weren't good parents, but no one's ever satisfied, I guess."

"I guess."

"Anyway," Rayne got to her feet. "I'll be back with sustenance."

Rayne went down into the galley and filled the kettle. She wasn't used to a propane stove, but she managed to light an element and felt quite proud of herself when the kettle began to boil. She spooned instant coffee into two mugs and tucked cheese between two bread rolls—leftovers from the picnic.

As soon as everything was ready, she carried the snack on a tray upstairs. Nick had finished the plugs and was testing wires. Still the air was dead calm, sort of stormy. Just what they didn't want was a downpour, Rayne thought as she put the tray between them on deck and sat down again.

Nick glanced at her preparations. "Thanks. It looks great. I'll eat this and then try to start the engine again. I think all it needed is routine maintenance."

"Where did you learn about fixing engines?" Rayne asked as they munched on the rolls and drank the coffee.

"My mother, believe it or not. We didn't always live in New York City. We used to live upstate, in a little country cottage. We had this old truck that was always going wrong. She knew how to get it going with a screwdriver. Then when I learned to drive, I had to have a car to get to town. And of course it was old and clapped out and needed constant repairs.''

''So you're not a city slicker?'' For some reason Rayne was rather relieved to know that. She'd been brought up in rural surroundings, as well, until her father had moved them to Flint.

''No.'' Nick drained his coffee. ''You're not either, I gather.''

''Small town in Michigan.''

''I thought you were from the city.''

''I moved to Chicago when I went to college and then I worked there until . . .''

''You came to the island,'' Nick finished for her. ''And you don't miss city life?''

''Not in the least.''

''Neither do I, tell you the truth.'' He wiped his hands on a rag. ''Now let's see if this thing will work.''

Rayne piled the tray with their empty dishes and took it down to the galley. She was about to return to the deck when she felt the rumble of the engine.

Nick was at the helm, packing away the tools.

Rayne shook away the disappointed feeling that the evening was almost over. ''You did it?''

''Magic.''

''That's great. Now no one will need to get worried about us.''

''I was thinking about that too. Do you want to steer while I get cleaned up?''

''Sure.''

They shared the helm on the way back. Rayne felt unusually placid and content, as if life couldn't get any better than motoring across the sea with Nick at her side, sometimes his hand bumping hers, seeing his white smile through the darkness. Tonight they had shared an intimacy removed from kissing and touching, and she could feel herself on the verge of falling in love with him. But she didn't want to question the experience. Not tonight.

Rayne spent the following morning editing the existing rate schedule and doodling some 'honeymoon' advertising ideas for the new season. She ignored the niggle at the back of her mind that if she had a personal computer to work on she would be better equipped to put together a presentation. But a computer was the last item they could afford right now.

The projected change in rates meant that she should consult Tanya, and in that event, Tanya would discover their inadequate financial situation.

With a huge sigh, Rayne pushed aside her idea pad. Maybe the time had come for Tanya to know the truth.

But she procrastinated about seeing Tanya by yet again moving her attention to the old files. She was still curious to know of any past offers Nick might have made.

As she went through the files, she discovered Larry had kept everything, and the hunt for L.R.E.'s proposal also became a clear out. Some items she would have to check with Tanya before she pitched them. So at lunchtime she finally went to see her sister-in-law.

Sean was at the desk, standing in for his mother.

"Where's your mom?" Rayne asked.

"I think she went upstairs to the suite. She said she wasn't feeling too good."

Feeling worried, Rayne hurriedly climbed the stairs to the second floor and ran along to the family flat. Tanya had been fine this morning. Had her first trip off the island been too much for her?

Rayne gently knocked on the door. "It's Rayne," she called out and pushed open the door. Tanya was sitting on a rattan sofa near the open door to the veranda. "What's up?" Rayne asked.

Tanya turned around. "You never told me that we didn't have much money, Rayne."

Feeling her legs buckle, Rayne closed the door and went to sit in the nearest chair to the sofa. "How did you find out?"

"Mr. Stinson called for you on my personal phone, so I took a message. He just wanted to know if you had come to any satisfactory resolution to our financial problems. And of course I asked him to explain further."

Rayne's stomach felt sapped of strength. This was the last way she would have wanted Tanya to discover that the resort was having financial problems. Mr. Stinson should have known better, but then again he believed that Tanya shared Rayne's knowledge. Rayne should have told Tanya long ago. "I've come up with a few cost-cutting ideas," Rayne said softly. "Don't worry about it, Tanny. It's only temporary."

Tanya gave her a sharp look. "Are you sure? You've been pretty antsy since you returned from Christmas vacation."

Rayne lowered her eyes for a moment. She'd always thought that Tanya was so wrapped up in her own grief that she wouldn't notice anyone else's moods. "I knew before I went home that we could get into difficulty. And the day I went over to Road Town I discussed our financial position with Mr. Stinson. He made some suggestions to reduce our outgoings and I've been considering them. And just this morning I put together a proposal for a rate increase."

"Does any of this make much difference?"

"The rate increase will, Tanya. I got this bright

idea last evening that we should aim our new fall advertising at couples—honeymooners. That way the rate raise won't seem too drastic.''

"Last evening? You were with Nick last evening, weren't you?''

"Yes, I was. That's when I got the idea. The meal we took with us was that honeymoon picnic. You know, the one that's on the bottom of the menu. Blink and you'll miss it. Well, I thought, why not capitalize on the honeymoon idea and offer complete packages. Make honeymooners more of an upfront item.''

Tanya gave her a funny look. "Why were you thinking about trying to keep the resort afloat when you were with Nick? Did he say anything to you?''

A tautness across Rayne's chest made her sound harsh. "Like what?''

"Like for instance, who he is. I'm asking because I've heard something unsettling. Someone told me that Nick Lewis runs a hotel management company. I mean, he might just be staying here for a regular vacation, but you don't think it's a little strange for the head of a big hotel chain to stay at our little family place?''

Rayne swallowed hard. She'd also never thought of Tanya discovering anything about Nick through the grapevine. "It is strange, I agree.''

"I'm merely warning you, Rayne. I wouldn't like to think he's making friends with us to suck us into any deal. You, especially. You've been with him quite a bit and I wouldn't want you to get hurt.''

"I've only been with him a lot because he's been paying attention to me. I've no intention of letting anything get out of hand.''

Tanya gave her arm a squeeze. "That's good. Although too bad in other ways, because I think you should be married and having babies by now.''

"But certainly not with Nick Lewis.'' Rayne forced a smile.

"No, not with Nick, even if his babies would probably be handsome children.''

"Tanya, it seems like he's sucked you in a bit.''

She nodded. "In some ways he's such a dear. I wouldn't have traveled off the island if it hadn't been for him. And he's got a famous mother. And I suppose if he is here with an ulterior motive, all we have to do, if and when he approaches us, is give him a firm no.''

"Exactly,'' Rayne agreed.

"And in the meantime, while Larry was always against raising rates too high, if it's our only answer, then I suppose we have to. The honeymoon package sounds quite nice. Also, Rayne, if you want me to take a cut, I will.''

Rayne felt relieved that Tanya had made that suggestion herself. ''Would you?''

''Sure, why not? I don't need all my allowance. I send away for far too many expensive clothes anyway. Now I'll be forced to go and shop for bargains in person. After all, I have been off the island once, I can do it again.''

''Of course you can. Oh, Tanny, thank you. That would help immensely. I'll revise the budget and reduce your income a little. Nothing too rash. Hopefully, the savings will get us over this bad patch and then when the revised rates and our honeymoon idea kick in about September we'll be in good shape.''

Tanya gave her a sideways look. ''This is why you're not that enthusiastic about Sean going back to college right now, isn't it?''

Rayne nodded. ''Partly. There isn't the spare cash. It would be a strain on the budget. And I really do think you need Sean here with you.''

''He's so much like Larry.''

Rayne leaned forward and laid a hand over Tanya's. ''I know.''

''Oh, dear, Rayne, this is worrying for you. I'm pleased it came out into the open. Why do you try to protect me?''

''Because you've needed to be protected.''

"Maybe in the past, but not anymore. I want to be strong." Tanya turned her hand and held Rayne's. "What happens if we can't pull out of this slump?"

"Well . . . Mr. Stinson thinks we should give any offers to buy the island serious consideration."

"Like Nick Lewis?"

"I think he's already approached Stinson."

"Oh, dear. This was Larry's place. Larry's dream. Everything that was Larry is here. No. That's completely unacceptable."

"I told Stinson that."

"Thank goodness. I mean, you do feel the same way, don't you, Rayne? We struggle rather than sell?"

"Absolutely. Why do you think I'm working on all these projects?"

"I know. You see, I couldn't leave Silver Island," Tanya said. "My home is here now."

"I'm not suggesting that you do leave. Neither is Mr. Stinson. He . . . we have to get into a more stable financial position, that's all."

"Which is mostly my fault."

"Not really," Rayne admitted. "I wanted you in a cocoon. And I was trying to upgrade the resort without raising prices."

"I suppose. But from now on you tell me what is going on. No hiding the facts, okay?"

Rayne nodded. "Okay."

"And if anyone wants to buy, remind them that you and I have to make the decision together. This place belongs to our family. Especially to Sean. If he's not going to college, the island is his future."

Rayne was pleased to see her sister-in-law acting so independently. "I'm on your side, Tanya."

The two women shook hands and they both stood up.

Tanya smiled. "Agreed, then. Now I'm going back down. I was feeling sorry for myself again and I mustn't get like that."

"You can come into the office and help me if you like," Rayne suggested on the way downstairs. "I'm going through some old files and I want your opinion on one or two of the items before I pitch them into the garbage."

"I'd love to help," Tanya told her.

Even with Tanya helping her check the correspondence, Rayne still didn't find anything from Nick and began to think that Nick might not have put anything in writing.

"Tanya, do you recall when Nick was on the island before?"

Tanya tossed away a package of obsolete advertising. "It was about a year before Larry died."

"Did Larry say why he was here?"

"No. Larry didn't talk to him much as far as I know. I remember Nick because he used to flirt with me at the pool."

Rayne smiled. "I bet."

Tanya grinned. "He's an extremely attractive man, Rayne. But he is a quite few years my junior. Even so, his attention is flattering. You know, though, when he was here before, he was a bit younger. He's maturing very nicely."

Not wanting to dwell on Nick's maturing good looks, Rayne stuffed some extremely out-of-date files in a box. "You see, I think he might have visited Silver Island at that time to approach Larry about his company buying the resort, and I'm looking for a letter."

"That initiated this clean-up?"

Rayne nodded and sat back on her heels. "But I haven't found anything."

"I don't remember Larry saying a word. People have always been trying to buy the place. Larry was against sales. If Nick approached him, I'm sure he would have been told where to go in no uncertain terms. You know what Larry was like."

"Yes, I recall how he could be quite obnoxiously adamant when he was convinced of something," Rayne grinned.

"Stubborn, like all the Sinclair family," Tanya said. "Sorry, Rayne, but every last one of you sticks to his or her convictions. Sean has inherited . . .'' Tanya stopped in midsentence as Sean came into Rayne's office. ''Hi, dear.''

''Hi, Mom. I didn't expect you to be in here. What are you two doing on the floor?''

''Tossing old files,'' Rayne said. ''You don't come in here much, either.''

''I thought I'd better let you two know that C. T. Lewis has arrived to stay.''

Nick's Mom! The writer who had written half of Rayne's own library, her favorite author, the woman who could invent men who looked just like her son, Nick; men who made women fall in love with them with the flick of an eyelash.

Rayne and Tanya both jumped to her feet and chorused, ''She's here now?''

Sean nodded. ''She hadn't booked, just arrived. Luckily Petunia was vacant. I've just taken her down. She's not at all like Nick. She has fair flyaway hair, an upturned nose, and a rosebud mouth. Nothing what I'd imagine a sci-fi writer to look like.''

''Does Nick know she's here?'' Rayne asked.

''Not yet. I put a call through to Nick to let him know she was here, but he wasn't in his villa. Then I searched the place and finally found out from Troy that he went fishing.''

''Fishing?'' Rayne echoed.

Sean nodded. ''On *Bright Sail*.''

''Really? So, if we can't find Nick, what shall we do about C. T. Lewis?''

''Why don't you go along and greet her, Rayne?'' Tanya suggested. ''You're the one who discovered her books. You sort of know her.''

''All right,'' Rayne agreed. ''I'll go. I don't need much persuasion to meet C. T. Lewis.''

''Take it easy,'' Tanya said. ''And enjoy yourself. I'll clean up in here. Sean can help me.''

To have her work taken over suddenly lifted a burden off her shoulders, and Rayne quickly went to the Petunia villa.

Chapter Six

Rayne found the villa door ajar and knocked softly.

"Come in," a woman's voice called.

Rayne poked her head around the corner. The fragile blond-haired woman was just as Sean had described her. She was sipping from a glass of water.

When she saw Rayne, she asked, "Is the water all right to drink here? I'm so thirsty."

"The water's fine," Rayne reassured her, thinking that the only physical resemblance she could spot between Nick and his mother was their eyes: deep sea blue, long-lashed, observant. "I'm the manager of the resort, Rayne Sinclair. I want

121

to welcome you to Silver Island to make sure you are settling in.''

"How nice of you. I'm fine, Rayne. . . .'' C. T. screwed up her forehead. "*Rayne*. Nick's mentioned you, I believe.''

Rayne didn't want to imagine what Nick might have said about her to his mother. Or why he should have mentioned her in the first place. "He has?''

C. T. put down the glass and moved forward with her hand outstretched. "Very definitely. In quite a favorable light, I might add. I'm pleased to meet you, Rayne.''

Rayne shook C. T.'s hand warmly. "And I'm pleased to meet you. I was really excited when I learned you were here. I've read all your books.''

"Oh, dear, a fan.'' C. T. gave a mock expression of dismay as their hands dropped.

"I won't bother you or anything.''

"I don't mind, truly. I'm only teasing. It's wonderful to know that people in all corners of the world read my work. And this is a beautiful place. Nick described it to me on the phone, and as I had just submitted my latest manuscript and was at loose ends, I decided I should come and see him. I wanted to surprise him.''

"I'm sure you will. I believe he went fishing. He shouldn't be too long.''

"Fishing? Nick? I didn't think he went for that type of sport."

"He's got a boat at his disposal. Belongs to a friend."

"Really? Well, I guess I'll wait." C. T. removed her tweed jacket. Beneath the jacket she wore a charcoal silk blouse. "It is hot, though, isn't it. Quite stormy."

Rayne hoped Nick would be all right on the sea if it did storm. A funny feeling caught in the pit of her stomach and lay there. Anxiousness. "It rained this morning. The rain doesn't usually last long."

"I don't mind rain. The entire Eastern seaboard is having an awful snowy cold winter. I wasn't unhappy to leave the mess behind."

"That's good. All you have to do here is kick back. That's what my nephew says, anyway."

C. T. laughed. "Kicking back describes what I want to do exactly. Nick tells me to do that sometimes. In fact, he's always at me about the way I work too hard."

"Me too," Rayne said.

"He gets on you as well?"

She nodded. "He thinks I overwork."

"It's because his father had a heart attack a few years back. He's slowed down himself since then. It changed his perspective on life, I believe."

There was a brief rap at the door. Rayne turned to see who was there. Nick poked his head around the corner. He looked flushed from the sun, and . . . agitated? But at least he was safe. Not out at sea in a storm. Rayne's worry subsided.

"Hi, Mom," Nick said, "I just heard you were here. This is a surprise."

"I'm supposed to be a surprise, Nick. Rayne's been helping me get settled in."

Nick's glance rested on Rayne. "Hi, Rayne. Thanks for taking over."

She smiled. "No trouble. Did you enjoy your fishing trip?"

"Yes. It was great. Didn't catch anything, though. Didn't intend to, actually. I was testing the motor on the boat."

"Did it work fine?"

"Purred like a kitten."

"Great." With a sad feeling that the intimacy of the evening before had dispersed, Rayne moved to the door. "I'll leave you two alone now. If you need anything, Mrs. Lewis, just call up to the desk. Sean, my nephew, will see you have what you need."

"Thank you very much, dear. And please call me C. T. Everyone does."

"All right, I will. It was a pleasure meeting you, C. T."

"It was a pleasure meeting you, as well. Why

don't you join us for dinner tonight and we can chat more?''

"Yeah, do that, Rayne," Nick said. "Invite Tanya and Sean too, if you want."

"If you're sure."

"Positive," C. T. said.

"Then I'd love to have dinner with you, C. T. Thank you. I'll ask the others."

Rayne closed the door softly. She had the impression Nick wasn't particularly keen that his mother had come to stay on Silver Island. Which was strange, when what he'd told her about his parents seemed to be that they'd neglected him.

A dinner date with C. T. Lewis took on larger proportions in her mind than Rayne would have thought earlier on. By the time she had showered and buttoned on an apricot rayon dress and put on cream sandals, she actually had butterflies in her stomach. After all, C. T. was extremely famous. Even if she'd had, as Nick had told Rayne, some lean years in her past, her books and sales were now purported to range in the millions.

Her jitters were also caused by Nick, who was slipping, very definitely, into her heart.

Rayne slipped some cash into her pocket for bar money—she rarely carried a purse or wallet on the island—and left her villa. She met Nick and C. T. on the way.

"Hi, there," Nick's Mom said cheerfully. "Nick has just shown me the marina and beach. Silver Island is an apt name. The sand *is* silver."

Rayne was very aware of Nick beside her, hands in the pockets of navy slacks, with which he wore a burgundy silk shirt. He appeared menacing, for some reason. Was he still disconcerted about his mother's sudden appearance? Or did he regret their evening together on the boat? She wasn't sure what his impression had been because they'd arrived back so late and had parted immediately. Had he regretted baring his soul to her?

C. T. coughed lightly and Rayne realized that Nick's Mom was awaiting a reply. "Yes, the sand does look like silver, especially near the end of the day, in the low sun." She sounded as if she were quoting from a travel brochure.

Nick shifted his stance. "Are you ready for dinner?"

Rayne met his gaze. "Yes. Are you?"

"Yes. But Mother just needs to pop into her villa once more. She'll meet us up at the hotel."

At the prospect of being left alone with Nick, Rayne's heart began to beat fast. "Fine with me."

C. T. left them and they continued walking together slowly, drenched in a long silence. They stopped, waiting for his mother to join them again.

Rayne bent and picked up a tangerine hibiscus blossom that had fallen on the path. She twirled it between her fingers.

Nick glanced at the bright orange flower, then at Rayne. "Tanya and Sean joining us?"

"Yes. If that's okay."

"They were invited."

"Yes, they were."

Nick shifted a little closer to her. "Look, Rayne. I have a problem."

At last, Rayne thought, he's going to tell me about wanting to buy the island. But why tonight? Is he worried his mother might say something? She realized then that she didn't want to know. She wanted to be left alone with her burgeoning feelings for Nick. "What kind of problem?" Her voice shook. Once she knew, there would be no turning back the clock, no more time like this with Nick.

"Are you all right?"

Rayne tossed the hibiscus to the ground. "Yes. I'm fine."

Someone cleared their throat behind them.

Nick and Rayne both twisted around to greet C. T., wearing a scarlet shirt-dress that made her pale skin glow.

C. T. said, ''I hope you haven't been bored waiting for me.''

''No. Not at all.'' Nick spoke in a breezy manner that was completely at odds with the strained words he'd just uttered to Rayne. With a magnanimous gesture he looped Rayne's arm with his, and then tucked his mother's, into his other arm. ''I can't wait to escort my two favorite ladies to dinner.''

Nick's problem wasn't revealed that evening or the next day. Rayne didn't see him. But she did see C. T., who popped unexpectedly into her office, much like her son had once done.

''Does anyone do tours of the resort?'' C. T. asked.

''Not on a regular basis, but I'll give you one if you want.''

''That would be wonderful. I'd like to know where everything is.''

Rayne spent a few enjoyable hours with C. T., showing her the resort's amenities. As a thank-you, C. T. autographed all of Rayne's precious books. Afterwards they sat on Rayne's veranda to watch the sun set and Rayne realized that the awe she'd felt in C. T.'s presence was slowly dissipating, and in its place a friendship was forming. Like Nick, C. T. was easygoing. Although, also like Nick, Rayne sensed a tenaciousness in the woman, a tenaciousness she'd possibly needed to keep going with her career.

"I haven't had a real vacation for so many years," C. T. told Rayne, "that this is absolute heaven. Do you like living and working here?"

"Very much."

"You don't mind the continual warm weather or miss the change of seasons?"

"Not at all. I'm from Michigan, where we have our share of cold. I don't long for winter one bit," Rayne smiled.

"You know, I think I might. This weather makes me want to laze around. Winter gives me energy and forces me to stay indoors and write."

"Your writing must take up a lot of time."

"Great chunks of time, Rayne, believe me. I've spent most of my life trying to make that time." C. T. ran her fingers through her fine hair. "Nick has never been very receptive to the time it takes. Mainly because I was never much of a mother to him. Which is why I felt I should make some space for him now."

"He's pleased about that."

C. T. glanced at Rayne. "Did he tell you that?"

"No. I just feel that he would be pleased."

"I haven't the foggiest notion if he is pleased or not. I get the impression he's on edge about something. But then Nick can hide his feelings quite adeptly. Just like his father. I don't know if Nick has told you anything, but his father and I had a rocky relationship. We divorced when Nick was fifteen, and I feel we stayed together too long even then. We used to go for days not speaking. Sometimes we'd separate physically. Craig would walk out, or I'd take my typewriter and go to a hotel room to work. Craig would come after me and we'd make up. I don't think I realized the impact on Nick until I was older, and maybe it was too late. But I was young and idealistic. And Craig wanted his marriage to be the way his parents' marriage was. You know, Mr. and Mrs. Perfectly Normal.''

Rayne smiled slightly.

C. T.'s return smile was rueful. ''Anyway, we got divorced, although neither of us has married again. Craig obviously hasn't found Mrs. Perfect, and I thought by not being married I would solve all my problems and have my freedom. I was wrong. At first I found I couldn't write much. It was as if the passion and unrest with Craig drove me to write. . . .''

C. T.'s hesitation gave Rayne a suspicion that Craig still meant a lot to her. And yet she knew from Nick that they hadn't seen one another since the divorce.

Nick's mother continued, ''Things did eventually get on track. I was able to send Nick to college. He was a bright boy, who excelled athletically and academically, and he's been successful.''

Rayne was waiting for C. T. to tell her what Nick had actually been successful at, but C. T. only yawned and patted her hand against her mouth. ''Excuse me, Rayne. It's getting past my bedtime. Would you mind if I left now?''

''No. Go ahead. I need to get to bed myself. I rise early to exercise before work.''

C. T. stood up. ''That sounds much too hectic in this heat, my dear. Thanks for the company, Rayne. Could you show me the route back to my villa? I'm a catastrophe at directions when I haven't had time to find my way by myself a few times.''

They left Rayne's villa together and turned up a sweetly scented lane. They reached C. T.'s villa. ''Thank you, Rayne.''

''Good night, C. T. Sleep well.''

''You too, and don't work too hard. You can miss out on a lot of life with your head buried in work.''

Did C. T. feel she had missed out, Rayne thought, as she returned to her own villa. From what C. T. had told her tonight, she had more than a few regrets about her broken marriage. Therefore, wasn't it better not to get involved with a man to such an extent that you put yourself

in a vulnerable position? Tanya was a good ex-
ample. Watching her sister-in-law struggle over
losing Larry had been difficult to watch. Even if
Tanya always said she'd forever treasure the time
she had with Larry.

Rayne closed her villa door and walked out
onto the veranda to pick up the glasses they had
been drinking from. Across the tangle of fauna
was Nick's veranda. Quiet tonight. Where was he
now? And why did she want to know when she
really felt it was better never to see him again.

The next morning, Rayne closed her office door,
huddled over the ledgers, and tried to create a
budget that would put the resort in good standing
with the bank. She added all her ideas for future
promotion and put an estimate of that income in
the budget.

By the afternoon, Rayne had two new files.
One, *Budget Ideas*, contained the proposed price
raise and the honeymoon plan. The other, *Budget
Cuts*, contained the savings from Tanya's expenses. Rayne had indeed found some significant
ways to cut the budget that would carry them,
barring emergencies, through to autumn. On her
way back to her villa to change for a predinner
swim, she crossed her fingers inside her skirt
pocket against any emergencies.

Rayne quickly changed into her black swimsuit, Nick's blue T-shirt, which had become a standard swimwear coverup, and a pair of sandals. Then, with a towel tucked between her fingers, she walked out to the freshwater pool. The water was sparkling blue and inviting after an afternoon spent poring over the stuffy ledgers. Rayne shed her shirt and sandals, tossed them on the side, and dove in.

Rayne swam for a long time before she eventually went to the edge of the pool and drew herself out. She toweled herself down, squeezed the water from her hair, and picked up her sandals and T-shirt.

Nick extended his bare leg and gently barred her way as she passed by. "Hi."

Rayne hadn't noticed Nick sitting under one of the umbrella tables. "Hi. How are you doing?"

"I wouldn't know. My heart's pounding so hard from watching you swim I can't think straight."

"Isn't that a coincidence? My heart's pounding so hard from contact with you that I can't think straight either."

Nick grinned. "Liar, but you can stay and have a drink with me."

Rayne moved away from Nick's outstretched leg and chose the chair across the table from him.

"What can I get you?"

"What are you drinking?"

"Light beer and lime."

"I'll have the same."

Nick left to get her drink and Rayne slipped on her T-shirt, then sank back in the chair to let the breeze and the sun dry her hair. Her eyes followed Nick, in khaki slacks and shirt, to the thatched bar. Against the other men laughing and talking on the stools, Nick's height and width of shoulder stood out.

Nick returned and placed a tumbler with a piece of lime attached to the rim in front of her. He sat down again.

"Thank you, Nick." Rayne peeled off the piece of lime and squeezed the juice into the beer. "Have you seen your mother today?"

"We're meeting on the marina later and going over to Fisherman John's. Want to join us?"

"I'm sure you would rather be alone with your mother."

"Not at the moment, because of that problem I never got to tell you about."

"Then tell me now." Rayne wasn't up for it, but she'd take it if she had to.

"Well, you know that my parents are divorced?"

"Yes."

Nick picked up a cocktail napkin. "And you know my parents haven't seen one another for quite a few years?"

Rayne nodded. This wasn't the problem she had expected.

Nick folded the napkin neatly. "Anyway, Dad is in the area on business and decided to visit me. He arrives on Saturday."

Rayne immediately took in the seriousness of the situation and leaned forward. "Did you know he was coming before your mother showed up?"

Nick fired the wadded napkin across the table. It ricocheted off the umbrella pole and back to Nick. He picked it up again. "Only that morning."

"I hope you've warned your mother."

"No. If I do that, she'll leave the island."

"Tell your father, then, and have him postpone his visit."

"I was thinking of doing that, but I'm sure he won't come at all, in that case."

"Nick, you can't have them both here at the same time. It's not possible to keep them apart on the island. For a start, there's only one restaurant."

"I've thought about all that. But I've also thought that I've always wanted them to get together again."

"Maybe you do, Nick, but they obviously don't want to be together." Rayne impulsively reached across the table and touched his arm to comfort him.

Nick put down the tattered napkin and covered her hand with his. "I'm not so sure about that. There's an old desk in my apartment in New York. My parents' names are carved on the top, in a heart. Mom said I was to keep it for her because she didn't have room in her apartment for it. Which isn't true. She's found room for other pieces of furniture that caught her eye; heck, her place looks like an antique store. I just don't think . . ." Nick stopped for a moment, as if to gain some composure. "Anyway, I just don't think C. T. has the capacity for the painful memories the desk would evoke if she used it at home."

Rayne glanced at Nick's hand. His flesh was marred by a few childhood scars, which added strength. The other scars didn't show. "Go on."

"So you see, at the back of my mind, I don't think they should be kept apart. It might be good for them to see one another and face the music."

"But you don't want to hurt your mother, Nick."

"I haven't done this intentionally. Neither one of them has exactly rushed to my side before. This is a first. And they both have to arrive at the same time."

Rayne smiled. "If it wasn't such a perilous situation, it would be funny."

Nick glanced at her. "What do I do?"

"You're asking me to make your decision for you? You run a success—" Rayne cut herself short. Nick had never told her what company he did run. If she let on she knew about him, then she would have to face his business deal. And she wasn't ready for it yet.

Nick didn't seem to notice, she stopped short.

"I helped you with Tanya. Not that I expected anything in return for that, but now I do."

"You should warn your mother."

"I don't want her to leave. She needs this vacation desperately."

"Then what do we do, Nick?"

"Stick together with my Mom as a couple, and then when Dad arrives on the weekend, we can help diffuse the situation somewhat."

"If necessary, Nick. They might be very civilized."

"I've never known my parents to be civilized about their relationship yet. Love does crazy things to peoples' heads."

I'll second that, Rayne thought.

Nick squeezed her fingers. "You're going to help me?"

"Yes. I'll help you."

"Great."

On Saturday Rayne was scheduled to take C. T. to Spanish Town on Virgin Gorda. Meanwhile

Nick had traveled to Tortola Friday evening, ready to meet his father at the Beef Island airport. Nick would then quickly whip Craig Lewis to Silver Island before C. T. and Rayne returned. They were both aware that a meeting between Nick's estranged parents would be inevitable, but Nick felt that at least they would be stationed on the island and would have to put up with one another. A theory Rayne wasn't too sure about.

C. T. changed her mind. She had been looking at the travel brochures and had decided that the shops at Road Town were probably more conducive for the gift buying she wanted to do.

There was no arguing with Nick's Mom once she'd made up her mind, and Rayne didn't know Nick's exact whereabouts, so that she could inform him about this change of plans. She just hoped that they wouldn't run into one another somewhere on Tortola.

Rayne and C. T. took off bright and early on the motor launch. The only other passengers on the sparkling morning were a couple and their young daughter, who sat opposite and occasionally smiled.

Knowing C. T. was weary, Rayne didn't bother with conversation. She merely enjoyed the summer-in-January day, always thankful for her chance to work and live in the B.V.I.

Upon arriving at Wickhams Cay, they stopped

for cold drinks at the same cafe that Rayne had been with Nick before. That trip seemed so long ago now.

"It's lovely here," C. T. said. "Sorry I'm not better company. The heat tires me out."

"It did me, at first," Rayne agreed. "Then I discovered that swimming kept me lively."

C. T. stirred her juice with a straw. "Yes. I must try swimming. Although I do believe I'm merely recovering from many years of work and my system is shutting down."

"You really should take more vacations."

C. T. smiled. "This one might just convince me."

Rayne returned Nick's mom's smile, thinking, *or make you reconsider ever taking a vacation again.* And she wondered how Nick was doing and if he'd met his father yet.

They did some shopping, C. T. purchasing a few items for friends back home, but Rayne could see that her heart wasn't in their expedition. C. T. was definitely exhausted.

After lunch C. T. admitted that she couldn't go on. "I think we should return to Silver Island so I can rest," she told Rayne. "If you don't mind?"

Rayne didn't mind in the least, if it meant they could return to Silver Island before Nick and his dad arrived.

C. T. collected her packages. "I think I just about have the energy to make it down to the marina," she said.

"All right. Hopefully, Troy will be there. If not, I'll contact him and have him pick us up."

"Good." C. T. smiled gratefully.

They took their time strolling to the marina. Rayne spotted the Silver Island launch right away. Troy was standing on the marina, hands on hips, legs apart, talking to two men. Both tall, obviously father and son—Nick and Craig Lewis.

Chapter Seven

Rayne wished she could have tossed a blanket over C. T.'s head and trundled her off. But C. T. had already seen the same scene as Rayne because she let out a gasp.

"Oh, no. No. Nick . . ."

Rayne pretended to act dumb. "What, C. T.?"

"The man with Nick is my ex-husband. Nick's father. How did this happen? We haven't seen each other for years and now we're miles away from home, and . . . No. Nick."

"It's not Nick's fault."

C. T. gave her a shrewd glance. "You knew about this?"

"Nick mentioned to me that his father was coming to the island. Yes."

"Why didn't you tell me? I would have left and gone to another island."

They were closing in on the men now. Troy glanced up and waved. Nick and Craig turned around. Craig was a tall athletic man like his son, except Craig's dark hair was sprinkled with silver in the sunshine. Nick gave Rayne a look of dismay and Rayne noticed that Craig had turned ashen beneath his leathery tan. She hoped the shock wouldn't hinder his weak heart.

"Hi, Mom," Nick said, and Rayne had to admire his control, his casualness, as if he met his parents after years of absence at Wickhams Cay every day of the week. But then he did head a successful company. He was used to manipulating situations.

C. T. reached for her son's arm. "Nick, what is happening? Craig . . . ?"

"Christina," Craig muttered in a hoarse voice.

Troy smiled at them all, innocently unaware of the tension. "Come on, ladies. Step aboard."

He helped C. T. and Rayne onto the boat. The two women sat down. C. T. whispered to Rayne, "I'm furious at that boy."

To have Nick described as a boy almost made Rayne laugh. Peak-of-the-absurd-situation hysterics, she supposed.

Nick and his father were now on the boat, seating themselves opposite the two women, in the place occupied by the other family this morning.

Nick tried to put some eye pressure on Rayne to respond to him. She knew what he was asking. She wasn't supposed to have come to Tortola today. So why had she changed plans?

Rayne shrugged her shoulders, indicating with her expression that all this had been his mother's idea. Not her fault. She would have to explain later. But she wasn't sure if Nick noticed her message.

Craig cleared his throat. "It's nice to see you, Christina. You look well."

"So do you, Craig." C. T.'s tone was as tight as a taut rubber band.

Nick leaned forward, hands on his knees. "Look, folks. I'll explain when we get to the island."

Rayne heard Nick's voice crack with emotion. There was a flush to his cheekbones. He was truly upset. This was a huge emotional moment for him. She wished she was beside him. She wanted to comfort him.

His father looked away from his son and his estranged wife. "I hope it's a good explanation."

"Then I'll explain now," Nick said firmly. "Both of you coming here was a surprise. I didn't have time to stop either one of you from arriving at the same time."

''You could have told me when you met me, Nick,'' his father sighed.

''And you certainly could have told me, Nick,'' his mother added. ''I've been here for a few days now. You told Rayne.''

''Okay, so I wasn't up front with either of you. Tough. It's about time you were both together, anyway.''

Craig grunted. ''I'm not having a family argument on this boat in front of Rayne.''

''Neither am I,'' C. T said.

Rayne felt as if she were listening to a soap opera that she felt guilty about watching because it was considered trash. She glanced away from them. The motor and the wind usually kept the person at the helm fairly contained, and if it wouldn't appear rude and unsupportive to Nick, she would get up and go and stand with Troy for the rest of the trip.

A silence had slipped over the Lewis family. Rayne was relieved, keeping her eyes focused on the distance, willing Silver Island to appear in front of them. When the lush growth and silver beach did finally emerge and they floated into the marina, everyone stood up at once, eager to disembark.

Once on dry land, C. T. strode away and Craig picked up his bags. ''Thanks, Nick.''

''For nothing,'' Nick muttered under his breath

as his father took off in the direction of the hotel, a different direction from his mother.

Nick glared at Rayne. "Why didn't you go to Virgin Gorda as planned?"

"Because your mother didn't want to go to Virgin Gorda. She decided her shopping would be better on Tortola."

He raised his arms in exasperation. "Couldn't you have persuaded her?"

"Your mother is strong-willed, Nick. What she says goes."

He pushed his hand through his hair until the thick strands stood up. "Aren't they a pair?"

"You knew what would happen."

Rayne saw disappointment in the slump of his shoulders and touched his bare arm. A spark of electricity jumped from him to her. "Things might not be as bad as you think they're going to be."

Nick slipped his arms around Rayne. "I hope so." His mouth found hers with ease, almost as if she had offered her lips to him. She must have offered them, because her arms were around his waist.

He released his mouth from her searching one and tightened his grasp around her, holding her, stroking her silky hair. "Sorry I was a jerk over you taking mother to Road Town."

"It's okay. I fully understand how you feel

about your parents and how they've affected you throughout your life.''

''That's wonderful.'' He kissed her once more. ''You've been great, Rayne.''

They drew apart.

Nick smiled at her. ''I'll go and see what's happening. I'll catch up with you later.''

''All right. And take care.''

Rayne walked away first, leaving Nick to meet the wrath of his parents.

Rayne couldn't relax after being with Nick. His kiss burning on her lips, she went to her villa, changed into a swimsuit, shorts, and T-shirt and took off for the beach. She was planning a swim in the rock pool but decided that she didn't feel like getting wet. All she felt like doing was walking while she tried to get her senses straightened out after an emotional day.

She was worried about Nick. Anxious to know how he would handle his parents' stay—*if* they stayed. She hoped they would, for his sake. He needed to have them here for a short time, so he could exorcise some of his childhood demons.

She was really hooked on Nick now. Gradually Nick had edged into her life and had become so much a part of it that she couldn't see beyond him being here, when she would once more be alone. Alone. She had never minded being alone before. And now she was wondering how she was going to cope.

"Rayne."

She turned around and saw Nick running with long strides after her. He caught up.

"Hi," he said breathlessly.

"Hi. How's it going?"

"They're both staying, that's a plus. It might be awkward at times, but the initial meet is over, so . . ." He shrugged.

Rayne could tell he was trying to act casual about something that was the core of his entire emotional outlook on life. "I'm pleased they're staying, for your sake. That's good."

Nick fell into step beside her. "I couldn't be this cool about it without you, Rayne. You've helped me get perspective."

"I haven't done much."

"Oh, yes you have. You've listened to something I've never actually put into words before. You've made everything seem clearer and less of a burden than I've made it out to be."

"I don't think you made it out to be a burden, Nick. It was a burden. I can tell when you talk about it."

"Ah, yeah. It was big stuff. But telling you about it has clarified a lot of things. I feel less emotionally embroiled. Almost as if I've got some distance at last and I can concentrate on my own emotions.'' He grasped her hand. ''You and me, for instance, Rayne. The other evening on the boat, I felt like we were drawing close to one another. Did you feel that way?''

Rayne stopped walking. Now what? Was this his final ploy? And yet she felt she had to be truthful. Everything that had passed between them couldn't be a lie, a game. ''Yes, I did.''

Nick let out a breath and slipped his hands beneath her arms, drew her to him, and lowered his mouth to hers.

Rayne placed her hands against Nick's chest, feeling a wall of unyielding muscle. Yet he kissed so sweetly with so much need.

When he released her, he smiled. ''It's early yet, but I feel a lot for you, Rayne.''

Rayne didn't know what to say. She wanted everything in the open between them, to see if he still spoke the same words to her.

''Do you feel that way?''

''I enjoyed the other night, Nick. It was fun. Compatible.''

''That's it?''

It wasn't it, but what could she say? *Nick, I know why you're here. I know why you want to be with me. What's the truth?*

Nick grasped her hand and they began walking again, their bare feet lapped by the low surf at the edge of the beach.

Something buzzed around Rayne's arm. She batted it with her hand. "Ouch."

"What's the matter, Rayne?"

"Something bit me."

"That was me."

"No, not you." Rayne was pleased he'd turned their kiss into fun. That way she might be able to dismiss it later when the truth of his visit came out. "This is on my arm."

"Likely a sand flea"

"Flea?"

He chuckled. "Not real fleas. Little sand bugs. *No-see-ums*. You telling me you haven't been bit before?"

"No, I haven't. I thought they were a local fairy tale that had no truth to it."

"Believe me, there's a whole lot of truth. Come to my villa, I have some witch hazel. They should be treated as they hang around longer than mosquito bites. Itch like crazy." Nick took hold of her hand again.

Rayne hadn't been in the Gardenia villa since Nick had occupied it. It was turned around the other way from hers, slightly smaller, with one bedroom. The bathroom was a pale ivory marble. Nick opened a bottle of witch hazel and soaked a cotton pad. Rayne extended her arm for treatment.

"You scratched it already."

"It itches, Nick."

"This'll help."

"Why didn't you get bit?"

Deftly he treated the bite. "Bugs don't like my blood."

"Why, what's wrong with your blood?" She shifted from foot to foot.

"Keep still. There's nothing wrong with my blood. I'm immune to bugs. It comes from spending a lot of time camping out when I was a kid."

"Who did you camp out with?"

"The neighbors. They had a boy about my age." Nick let go of her arm. "How does it feel now?"

"It still itches."

"Take this bottle then. And please don't scratch it. The bite I mean."

Rayne smiled as she took the bottle from his hand. "Thank you."

"I can't understand how you haven't been bit before."

"I usually avoid wearing perfume when I go to the beach. Today I just changed without taking a shower. I guess I attracted the little beasties."

Nick ushered Rayne out of the bathroom and into the sitting room. The veranda door was open and a nice cooling breeze blew through. There was a pile of paperbacks on the table, a briefcase, and a pocketbook computer that would have looked like another briefcase if it wasn't opened with the sunlight reflecting on the blank screen.

"That's the first time I've seen a computer on this island," Rayne commented, walking over to the table. She touched the neat computer, forming an idea of how to snare him at his game, to make herself realize what a creep he really was and thus get him out of her system. Because it was difficult when he kept being so nice to her. She cleared her throat. "Did you, er ... bring work with you?"

"I often have a few things to do away from the office."

"You know, Nick, after all we've done together, I still don't know what you do for a living. Your mother said you were successful, and you seem to be able to please yourself by taking a month's vacation here."

"I own a company named Lewis Recreational Enterprises."

"And what does Lewis Recreational Enterprises do, Nick?"

His gaze met hers. "You know that already, don't you? You've known it all along. You almost told me earlier today but you cut yourself off."

It had been a strain waiting for Nick to acknowledge his real reason for being on Silver Island. Especially the way he'd led her on by being so nice, by kissing her, by complimenting her. At least she had kept some perspective. "Yes, I do, and you don't have to ask the question you've been courting me to ask, because the answer to your question is no."

Nick let out a long sigh. "I knew that, Rayne. That's the truth of why I haven't said a word. I mean, you're hanging on to a dead man's dreams for dear life. You'd sink with the ship if you had to."

"Exactly. You've got the picture."

"In living color, honey. But I think you're being short-sighted."

"No, I'm not. I've fixed the budget with some cost-cutting, and I also have some great ideas lined up for next season that will bring in more resources. Besides, we're not exactly down to our last dime. Larry wanted to be self-supporting. So do I. You should understand that."

"I understand that. What I don't understand is idealism that borders on stupidity. Your brother's dream is fading, Rayne. You know that. The bank certainly knows it."

"And that's another thing, Nick. You went to the bank and told them your intentions behind our backs."

"I deal with that bank and they've known for years that I've been interested in acquiring Silver Island."

''And they're on your side, naturally.''

''They're on the side of secure money. And you haven't heard my offer yet. It's a lot of money.''

His tenacity infuriated her. ''I'm not interested in making a lot of money and walking away from something that means so much to me. Don't you realize by now that I don't want to hear it? I just want you to do what the other guests do—vacation. Or leave.''

''Have you talked to Tanya about this?''

''Yes. She knows why you're here. The gossip on this island is something else. Nick, it's not on.''

''I don't see how you can say that when you haven't seen my offer.''

''Nick, give up. Thank you for the witch hazel. I'll return the bottle when the bite goes away.''

''Keep it. I'll get another bottle.''

His clipped tone cooled Rayne's trip out into the hot sun. She strode to her own villa. Well now the reason he was here was out in the open. Finally.

She went into the bathroom, put some more witch hazel on her itchy bite, and gazed at her tortured features in the mirror. Did the exposure of Nick's offer end any more intimacy and good times between them? Likely, it did, and she bit back the surge of disappointment. Again she wondered, as she had earlier, how she was ever going to cope.

She coped. By stuffing Nick's written offer into her top drawer without bothering to read it.

She coped. Because she didn't see Nick. He was probably playing the juggler, entertaining his mother and father. She did know he went to another island with Sean to play golf. Obviously, as she'd already decided, he wouldn't want her now that he knew her negative answer. There was no more motivation to make her fall in love with him.

She also coped with the office work as she tried to turn Silver Island into a honeymoon haven. And that wasn't hard. Silver Island was a natural paradise, a lovers' haven.

Yes. They'd do fine, she was sure. They didn't need Nick Lewis.

Tanya popped her head around Rayne's door. "You haven't had lunch yet, Rayne. It's almost two o'clock."

"I'm not hungry."

"You haven't been hungry for days. You must have lunch. There's not that much work, surely. We're not full by a long shot."

"That is the main problem, Tanya. I'm working up an advertising brochure for the autumn. So we will be full."

Tanya tapped her polished fingertips against

the doorpost. "I saw Nick this morning. He said he'd given you an offer. He asked me to read it."

"That man doesn't give up."

"May I read it?"

"Why bother? We're not accepting."

"Have you read it?"

"No."

"Well, I'd like to, Rayne. I don't like what our lack of finances is doing to you. It'll make you ill. Let me see it."

Tanya walked into the office with her arm outstretched. Rayne sighed and opened her top drawer. She handed Tanya Nick's folded letter in the pristine envelope.

"Thank you." Tanya slid the letter into her skirt pocket. "Now come for lunch."

Rayne smiled slightly. "This sounds like me to you a few months ago."

"You helped me, I'll help you. You can't get run-down, especially when you've been so much help."

Rayne acquiesced and stood up. She could do with a cup of coffee, at least.

They walked into the Bay View. Nick was there with his mother having a drink. C. T. waved and smiled. Nick saluted solemnly.

Tanya and Rayne chose a table a short distance away from the others. Rayne hadn't seen Nick for so long that her eyes became greedy for the sight of him. She was now going to do a count-down till the day he left. That day would mark her emotional freedom.

''Nick says he's having quite a time,'' Tanya told Rayne when their coffee had been served along with a cheese, pâté, and fruit plate. ''What with both parents here.''

''He asked for it. He didn't warn either one that the other would be here, so they ended up together.''

''He says they're staying for him, not for one another.''

Rayne stirred her coffee. ''That's true, and it's good they did stay. He had a hard childhood.''

''Did he tell you that?''

''Yes. He's told me.''

''You're really close, aren't you?''

''No. We're not close. He did what he had to do to try and get us to sell the island.''

''You think he was using you?'' Tanya frowned.

''Exactly. What else?'' Rayne glanced up at that moment and saw Nick looking at her. Her hand trembling, she dropped her spoon onto the saucer.

Tanya winced at the clatter she made. ''Rayne, are you feeling okay about Nick?''

''I'm feeling fine. Nothing has anything to do with Nick.''

"Yes, it does. You two make a great couple. You seem well-suited. But regardless of Nick, you must take it easier. You'll make yourself ill.''

"I'll take the weekend off.''

"You do that. I'll lock your office door.''

Rayne knew she would. The old Tanya was reappearing with a vengeance.

They were partway through their lunch when Nick and C. T. came over to their table. Nick lounged in a chair and C. T. perched on the edge of another.

"I want a way to get around the island, other than on foot,'' C. T. said. "Any ideas?''

"You can't drive,'' Tanya told her, "the tracks are too narrow. We have some bicycles. We used to rent them when my husband was alive, but . . . somehow they've been forgotten. I could have my son look them over and make sure they're in shape. Rayne used to cycle a lot when she first visited here. Didn't you, Rayne?''

Rayne nodded.

Nick looked in Rayne's direction. "Now she works too hard to have time for such frivolity.''

Rayne heard his sarcastic edge and gave him a cool smile. "I do other things instead, and I'd forgotten about the bicycles. True.''

"Would you be willing to be our guide on Saturday, Rayne?'' C. T. asked. "It would be nice to have you along for the ride, so to speak.''

"I haven't . . ."

"Go, Rayne," Tanya urged. "You're having the weekend off, remember?"

"And we'll pay big bucks," Nick put in.

"We wouldn't expect you to pay," Tanya told him.

"Goodness yes," C. T. said. "Especially if you have to get the bikes in shape. We'll need four."

"There are six," Rayne said, wondering why they would need four. Nick, C. T. and herself made three.

C. T. smiled. "Then it's all taken care of?"

Tanya nodded. "Sure. I'll talk to Sean."

Nick left to help Sean, and C. T. went to her villa. Rayne looked at her sister-in-law. "I thought Nick was the enemy. And now you're pushing me in his direction and being nice to him."

"He's also a guest, Rayne. So is his mother, who's famous, in case you've forgotten, and if they want bikes, then they shall have bikes. There are some beautiful sights on the island, you know that."

"Tanya, you are really becoming strict."

"It's about time I took some of the load off your shoulders. You go on Saturday, Rayne, and have a good time."

Rayne felt she had no choice.

Chapter Eight

Rayne hadn't cycled on the flat sandy island trails for at least a year, but she remembered the way to her favorite beach.

Both C. T. and Craig had cameras with them and every once in a while they all had to stop to give them time to take pictures of a bright bird, an interesting tree, or a cascading waterfall.

"I bet we're going to see some of this in a book one day," Rayne commented as they mounted their bikes again. "But I'm sure you'll project Silver Island into the year two thousand and fifty or something."

"It'll pop up, I'm sure," C. T. told her. "How am I ever going to get back to work again? I'm beginning to enjoy not doing anything."

"Me too," Craig intercepted. "I'm considering an early retirement."

Nick's strong bare legs were astride his bicycle, his feet planted on the sandy path. "Why not, Dad? You've had one heart attack. You don't want to be one of those guys who drops dead the day after retirement. You should enjoy life."

"That's a new attitude for you, son. You haven't exactly relaxed since you graduated college."

"I had a plan," Nick told his father. "I wanted to make enough money so I didn't have to work too hard for the second half of my life. And mother, you don't have to."

"I have fans, Nick. They expect a C. T. Lewis novel on the shelves at least once a year."

Rayne laughed. "One isn't enough for me."

"See, she's the type of avid reader that I'm up against." C. T. grinned and settled on her seat once more. "Come on, let's find that beach and have our picnic. All this fresh air is making me hungry."

Seldom-used muscles ached in Rayne's legs by the time they reached the beach. They all set down their bikes and collapsed onto the fine white sand. The area was open, the beach resting alongside an outcrop of low vegetation. White rocks crawled into the turquoise sea.

"It's like a desert island," C. T. exclaimed. "Beautiful. Isn't it, Craig?"

"Beautiful," Craig said, but Rayne noticed that he was looking at his ex-wife, not the view.

Nick opened the hotel-prepared lunch. A bottle of wine and fresh fruit accompanied the rolls stuffed with seafood and chicken. They sat in silence, munching, enjoying the sound of the surf breaking against the rocks.

Rayne had to admit she needed this break. And she was enjoying the family atmosphere. Well, semi-family, she corrected herself. Each of the Lewis family was self-contained. Unlike her family, who bounced off one another, the Lewises could be considered separate entities.

C. T. let some fine sand drift through her fingers. "Anyway, I'm going to walk off the lunch by taking a little jaunt along the beach. Anyone want to come?"

C. T. got to her feet.

Craig eased himself up. "I'll come with you, Christina."

Rayne and Nick both watched the blond woman in a blue sundress and straw hat and the tall silver-haired man in white shorts and shirt stroll away from them. Rayne thought how the holiday had changed C. T. She'd arrived drained and tired. Now she seemed to have a wealth of youthful energy to burn.

Rayne mentioned this to Nick.

"It's good to see. Especially good to see them together."

Rayne heard the crack of emotion in his voice. She nodded. "It is good. Wouldn't it be romantic if they remarried?"

"Let's not go that far. They might be better off being friends and living apart."

Rayne picked up a shell. The delicate pearly form was cool against her warm palm. "You seem have to come to terms with their relationship."

"I have. It's Silver Island. It works magic." He leaned on his side and ran his finger over her knee. "And you. I told you. You've helped admirably."

Rayne's breath caught in her throat from his touch. "That's good."

"You don't believe me, do you?"

"You came to the island with a mission, Nick." Rayne tossed aside the shell, wishing she could toss aside her emotions as easily.

"And I suppose in your mind that cancels out everything between us?"

"Naturally it does. You want Silver Island, Nick. Not me."

"I'd like both, actually."

"Well, you're not getting both." Rayne stood

up, making his hand drop from her knee. "I'm going to test the water."

Rayne ran to the edge and waded out a little way until the tepid water covered her ankles. Azure waves leapt over rocks and crashed in white foam. Her breathing quickened. She glanced back and saw Nick standing in the low surf, hands in the pockets of his shorts.

"Why do you have to be so stubborn, Rayne?"

"I'm not stubborn. I'm preserving my territory. Why should I cave in?"

Nick joined her and stood beside her, kicking the sand beneath his feet and watching the clouds form in the water. "That's true, I suppose. Why should you cave in?" He slipped his fingers into hers and tugged her to face him.

"Your eyes are like the sea, so green," he whispered and lifted her chin.

Rayne pulled away from him. "Hold it, Nick. You're not going to get to me that way."

"I'm not trying to get to you. All I want to do is kiss you again."

"I don't want to kiss you."

"Well then, if you don't want to kiss me, we'll get down to business. Have you read my offer yet?"

"No. I haven't. And I won't." Didn't the man have the word NO in his vocabulary?

Nick shook his head. "I can't believe you. We

could have it all. You and I.'' He turned around
and walked through the water up to the beach.

Rayne closed her eyes for a moment. She
needed strength to continue.

Luckily, C. T. and Craig's appearance put an
end to any more discussion. C. T. and Craig
wanted a short rest and a drink of pop before they
all packed up the picnic and began the trip back
to the resort. If Nick's parents noticed that Nick
and Rayne didn't speak to one another, she didn't
care. All of the Lewis's and their problems would
soon be gone from Silver Island and the Sinclair's
could get on with their lives.

Tanya and Sean were at the hotel to greet their
arrival back, so Rayne had no trouble escaping
Nick. She returned to her villa, stripped off her
shorts, shirt, and underwear and stepped under
the shower. Cool, refreshing water, that's what
she needed. Hot and bothered was a term she
hadn't used much until she had met Nick.

She was tying the belt of a peacock green silk
robe when Tanya arrived at the door.

''Hi. Are you tired?''

''It was a lot of pedaling my legs weren't used
to.''

''I bet. C. T. said it was a great day. I just want
to talk to you.''

''Let's get some drinks and sit on the
veranda.''

Rayne poured two juices and carried the glasses to the veranda.

Tanya smiled. "I forget how lovely it is here sometimes. You know, you get to rushing around and don't appreciate where you are."

Rayne handed Tanya her drink and kept her own. "I always appreciate where I am every morning when I take to the beach."

Tanya sat with her back to the view. "You're so energetic. But I think you're getting worn out. I read Nick's offer, by the way."

"You tossed it, I hope."

"No. I'm actually considering it."

Rayne let out a harsh sigh. "Tanya. Don't let Nick Lewis get to you. He's got all the charm in the world to work magic." *And I should know,* she thought.

"This isn't anything to do with pressure from Nick, this is my own common sense. I was in the office looking over the ledgers this afternoon and I'm no accountant, but it's obvious you've been doing some very skillful juggling to keep us afloat."

"I'm good at that."

"I know, but how long can you go on?"

Rayne took a drink and cradled the icy glass. "Look. I told you. I have plans for a honeymoon package. We'll have to spend a little extra on advertising, but . . ."

166 *Jillian Dagg*

''That's the point, Rayne. We haven't got the extra to spend on advertising. Nick's offer is not a buyout, as I at first thought. His company will buy shares, enough to keep us solvent.''

Rayne narrowed her eyes. This sounded too good to be true. ''What about our shares?''

''We keep them. I'll still have the fifty percent plus and the final say.''

''For how long, Tanya? I know these types of deals. Before you can blink a few times L.R.E. will be the controlling voice.''

''I won't let it. We'll write up a contract.''

Rayne took another sip of her drink. It would also mean that Nick Lewis would never be out of her life. Could she live with that? ''Tanya, let me read his offer before you go making a fool of yourself.''

This time Tanya's eyes narrowed. ''I am not making a fool of myself, Rayne. Just because I was weakened by Larry's death, doesn't mean to say I've lost my brainpower or my sense. And you can talk about being a controlling voice. I love you, Rayne, but sometimes you just have to back down a little, give a little. You would have learned that if you'd ever been married, especially to a man like your brother.'' Tanya walked over to her sister-in-law and touched her shoulder. ''You can't be perfect, Rayne. We don't expect you to be. So read Nick's offer and together we'll make a decision. I've left the letter on your desk with my opinions on little blue Post-It notes.''

Rayne's eyes filled with tears. ''You must have been a great wife to Larry. No wonder he adored you.''

''We had our moments.'' Tanya smiled sadly. ''But it's over, Rayne. John Barth has invited me over to Fisherman's for an evening out with him and I've accepted.''

''You have a date with John Barth?''

''Yep. He phoned me this afternoon.''

''That's wonderful.''

''It's a start.'' Tanya lifted her glass. ''So here's to us and continued success.''

Rayne lifted her own glass. ''To continued success. To your newfound freedom. Have fun.''

''I'm planning to,'' Tanya told her. ''But I don't want too many money worries to mar my fun. And I want to stay put as well, not because I'm scared to leave the island, but because I love it here. I don't want us to get down to the line and then be forced to sell to someone less honorable than Nick.''

''I agree with that,'' Rayne said.

''Anyway, Larry's been gone for a long time now and we both have to make a few adjustments. Read Nick's letter.''

After Tanya had gone, Rayne's glance drifted

across her veranda to Nick's. She remembered the evening she had stood here and spied with her binoculars. So long ago, it seemed, but in reality only a few weeks. At that time she'd felt so secure, so sure of herself. Now she felt as if sand was shifting beneath her feet, her entire existence changing shape. Nothing stayed the same, she thought. With Tanya and Sean she had carved out a life so they could all protect themselves while they recovered from Larry's death. Now that Larry's death wasn't so prominent, they all had to begin living again. Tanya most of all. But also Rayne had to make changes. She hadn't realized how stagnant her life had become, even when sharing it with this beautiful island.

Restlessly, she rattled the last of the ice cubes in her glass. She used to feel settled. She'd told Nick that. But settled was the last thing she felt, now that Nick had shown her heaven. Rayne eased an ice cube into her mouth and sucked on the frozen water. Nick had ruined her feelings for any other man. And now Tanya wanted to collaborate with him. Bring him into their select circle. And she'd likely have to deal with him for the rest of her life. Unless she gave up the management of Silver Island to Tanya and went home. She could get a job back in Chicago, or even Flint, rent an apartment, and begin again.

But the thought of doing that depressed her. It

was a change she didn't truly want with all her heart.

Rayne read and reread Nick's letter the next morning. Yes, sure, she thought, this sounded good. A great offer, leaving the Sinclair family still in control. This was Nick showing diplomacy, tact, and definitely manipulation. She'd like very much to see the first proposal he'd planned for them. She bet it was a straight buyout.

She tucked the letter into her desk drawer. Tanya was now convinced this offer from L.R.E. was what they needed to keep going. But she wasn't. Not by a long shot.

Of course it would be easy to succumb. She cared about Nick. She didn't want him to leave. But did Nick really care about her? He said she'd helped him get a perspective on life, but was that enough?

No.

She wanted him to love her, the way she loved him.

All she had was one week left with Nick on Silver Island.

She had to see him at least some of the week. That would be easy enough. All she had to do was pretend she wasn't mad at him anymore.

Rayne pushed back a heavy lock of her hair.

Everything felt weighty today. She needed to leave the office, see Nick.

So that no one would see her, Rayne escaped via the veranda. Once outside, she thrust her hands deep into her pockets and coiled her fists. She'd never felt so incomplete in all her life, so absolutely lost . . . without Nick.

Rayne made her way down the path, her attention on the job at hand, because the path could be treacherous if one didn't watch their step. But she couldn't help her gaze straying to the view. The misty hump of islands, the azure brilliance of the Francis Drake Channel. Around her, flowers, in all shades of red and pink, almost blinded her with their beauty.

A beauty that intensified when she was with Nick.

She slipped into the tropical shade of the pathway that led to Nick's villa. Taking a deep breath, she rapped on his door.

A beauty that would dull when Nick was gone.

She rapped again. Don't say he wasn't here. Not when she wanted to see him so much.

He obviously wasn't there. And who would be squirreled away in a villa on such a beautiful day?

''Isn't he in?''

A voice similar to Nick's made her jump. ''Hi, Mr. Lewis.''

"Hi." Craig Lewis smiled. "You seem edgy. Working too hard?"

"Everyone thinks I do."

"You give that impression."

"Well, it's true." Rayne pushed her hands into her skirt pockets.

"Then come for a walk along the beach with me. I feel like some company."

Rayne joined Nick's dad for his walk. Both the Lewis men were intent on her relaxing. Although she would never relax again properly. Not without Nick in her life. It was going to be terrible after he left.

"It's wonderful here," Craig said. "I'm pleased I came and pleased I stayed."

"Even given the circumstances?"

He gave a deep chuckle. "Even given those. It was actually good to see Christina again. I've always wanted to, but denied myself the pleasure."

"Then things are okay. You're not mad at Nick anymore?"

"No, I'm not mad at Nick. Although he took a bit of a risk. But then, that's Nick. He's more like his mother. He goes out on a limb. I'm more conservative."

"Me too," Rayne said. "I like to be sure of something before I venture in."

"Then you're not going to take a risk with Nick?"

"Do you mean the island?"

"No. I meant the two of you. I thought you made a pretty good couple." Craig glanced at her. "I know about the island deal. Nick told me. If you think he might be ignoring you since then, then Nick could be playing it safe."

"What do you mean by that?"

"Well, he could be a little afraid of his emotions, the way he feels about you. I was so frightened I might be hurt beyond description and that I wouldn't be able to handle that hurt that I was never able to keep any relationship going for long."

"But you did handle hurt," Rayne said. "You're here to prove it."

"That's true, I suppose, but I feel that I took the coward's way out. If Christina had been a different type of woman, she might have hung on. But she had aspirations other than a healthy marriage."

"So you let her go?"

"She needed to go. I stifled her. Anyway, it's all over now. And we're friends again. Thanks to Nick and this great island."

"Silver Island is like that, cathartic." Rayne told him with a smile. "I'm pleased."

"It would make me pleased, and Christina, if you and Nick . . ."

Rayne didn't respond but she thought about

Nick's father's words for the rest of the day. Was Nick's reluctance to pursue their relationship because he was afraid of being hurt, or was he merely ambitious, a person who would give up any relationship that didn't further his business endeavors?

Oh, forget about him, Rayne. The office still needs running. You have to be able to live your life the way you've always lived it. Before Nick.

Rayne exercised the following morning with a vengeance, swam double her laps, and then, after her shower, dressed in one of her prettiest dresses. She ate breakfast with Sean and Tanya on the terrace and felt resolved to be herself. To be normal.

"Did you get a chance to read Nick's letter?" Tanya asked when they were walking toward the hotel after breakfast.

"I've been busy, Tanya, but I glanced at it."

"Good deal, don't you think?"

"I haven't decided yet. It could be a sucker play."

"Not if we're smart."

"Give me more time," Rayne said.

Tanya sighed. "You know, C. T. and Craig are leaving tomorrow. We're all having dinner together tonight."

Rayne's gut reaction was that she couldn't face a dinner with Nick there. Then how were you going to face him, to see him the rest of his time here, you dolt? "Fine. Just let me know the details."

"Details? Rayne what is up with you?"

Rayne felt tears quiver behind her eyes. She was on the verge of breaking down. "I never asked that of you," she said huskily.

"Because you knew what was up with me. I know you're worried about the future of Silver Island, but I'm sharing that with you now. It's something else. It's Nick, isn't it?"

"Nick's a pain in the . . ."

"You love him."

No. Don't say it aloud. Rayne swallowed hard.

Tanya placed her hand softly on Rayne's arm. "Don't let stubbornness mess up your life. I'm willing to negotiate with Nick on the Silver Island business. You're free to go to him. And Rayne, if you marry him, then he's one of the family and the island hasn't left us, has it?"

Rayne hadn't thought about the situation in that light. If she married Nick. But she wasn't going to marry Nick. He didn't love her. He'd used her. "We're not going to get married, Tanny. We're not even in love. . . ."

Tanya patted her. "Well, whatever happens, don't put the island up as a barrier to him. Please."

Rayne blinked away her tears.

With a last squeeze, Tanya departed.

Rayne walked into her office. One last dinner party with the Lewises this evening. They would leave. Then Nick. She didn't doubt that Nick would leave.

Chapter Nine

Passionate island rhythms throbbed in the air. A group from Spanish Town supplied entertainment for the evening. Entertainment, they'd found, on the brief occasion when they could afford it, kept guests at their tables after dining, buying rum punches.

All the ice had melted in Rayne's rum punch by now. Her meal, although light, settled in her stomach like a lead weight. Besides Nick, his mother and father, Tanya, and Sean, John Barth and his daughter, Felicia—the girl who had danced with Sean at Fisherman John's the night of Tanya's party—had made a surprise visit over on their yacht.

Tanya's birthday seemed light-years away, and

yet it had only been a couple of weeks. Two weeks for Tanya to break out of her shell. Or was it that she had been breaking out all along and Rayne's step backward to give her space had allowed her to fully open up? She had Nick to thank for that.

Rayne felt him looking at her and she dropped her gaze into her drink. She'd heard him tell Tanya that *Bright Sail* was docked at Silver Island once again. He'd given both his mother and father trips around the islands. He didn't speak directly to Rayne. They hadn't passed a word since the bicycle picnic.

The music ended, the two musicians stopping to take a break. Everyone clapped for more, which would come later. A pause in time for Rayne to plead weariness and return to her villa. She stood up from her chair.

"It's good night from me," she said.

C. T. also stood up. "Oh, dear. I'll be gone early in the morning, so I'll say good-bye now, and hope to see you again one day."

"Silver Island will always be here." *And so will I,* Rayne added. Nothing was going to drag her away.

"And I've got five books to write," C. T. smiled. "But I realize that a vacation now and then really refreshes the soul. Remember how exhausted I was at the start?"

Rayne nodded and the two women drifted together and hugged.

"Look after yourself, Rayne. And my son," she whispered.

Or maybe that wasn't what she said, Rayne thought after she'd bid good night to everyone else and was on her way to her villa.

She heard the music start up again, pulse through the air, float over the island. She wasn't really tired. She was strung like a taut wire. All she'd do in her villa was pace the floor or toss and turn if she went to bed. Instead she walked to the marina. Lights twinkled on islands. The breeze from the sea was fresh and cooling.

Bright Sail sat in the same berth it had been docked in before. She stroked the smooth blue and white hull and then turned to see Nick beside her, wearing the short-sleeved navy shirt of the evening, with pressed white slacks. Sometimes the humidity played with his thick hair and curled it. Or was it that he hadn't had a haircut and his hair had grown in the month he'd been here?

Swallowing hard to compose herself, Rayne smoothed her flowing white pants and orange top. "Hi. Dinner finished?"

"Yep. I just saw mother to her villa. I'm taking her over to Beef Island on the yacht tomorrow." He thrust his hands into his pockets.

"Your friend certainly never uses the boat, does he?"

Nick shook his head. "Never. So I'm buying *Bright Sail*."

"You had to go home with something, I suppose."

He shifted his feet. "You mean, no island, but I have a boat?"

Rayne nodded, her fingers tracing the boat's name painted on the side.

"Tanya is agreeable, it's now up to you. I bet you haven't even read my letter."

"I did as a matter of fact, but . . ."

"You're not going to back down."

"How do I know that I can trust you?"

Nick took his hands out of his pockets. "If you don't know that by now, Rayne, you're never going to know. And how do I know I can trust you . . . you spy?"

"What do you mean?"

"The first night you came home and stood on your veranda and peered at me through binoculars."

Rayne's flesh turned warm all over. "You saw me?"

"Yep."

"I thought you might have, but when you didn't mention anything, I thought—"

"You thought you'd gotten away with it."

Rayne flipped her hand dismissively. "I just wanted to see who you were. I heard rumors about you."

"Which turned out to be correct?"

"Yes. Because I'm positive your initial offer was not your final offer."

"You're right. I wanted everything, lock, stock and barrel. I'm a rotten guy, huh?"

Rayne glanced away from his brilliant stare. "Well, not really. You backed down for some reason."

Nick sighed deeply. "For a good reason. Do you want to go for a boat ride and I'll tell you why?"

"It's late."

"Who cares? We're in a tropical paradise. A playground."

True. All true. And really, could she face being alone tonight without Nick? She'd planned on spending more time with him. Why not tonight? And then in a few days he'd be gone and she'd be fine.

"Let's go then."

While Rayne boarded the boat, Nick unfastened the chain and joined her. He fired the engine and took off out of the marina.

"No sails?" she asked.

"No. There isn't time. I want to get somewhere where we can be alone."

So did she.

He ended up on the other side of the island, the place where they'd eaten the honeymoon picnic. He stopped the boat, shut off the engine, and anchored.

Rayne leaned on the rail. The full moon illuminated the water and flickered across to the mound in the sea that was Silver Island. Larry's Island. Tanya's island. Her island . . .

"I'm not going to take the island away from you," Nick said behind her. "I'm not going to destroy your life. But if you don't give a little, Rayne, you're going to destroy my life."

She turned her back to the railing. "You mean, the failure of not getting what you want, namely the island?"

His gaze stayed riveted on hers. "No. I don't mean that. I've handled business failures before. L.R.E. hasn't been immune to recessions or the global economy. I had to sell two resorts that weren't making money."

"But you didn't lose everything you love by selling those resorts. That's what you don't understand, Nick. Silver Island is it. We only have one resort."

He moved closer to her. "You're not going to lose everything, Rayne. Neither is Tanya, or Sean. I'm on your side."

Rayne dropped her eyes from his. She stared

at her hands. Was that the truth? She certainly
heard sincerity in his voice. She wanted to believe him desperately. ''Tanya told me not to put
the island as a barrier between us.''

''Then don't.'' He reached out and gently
lifted her hair. His fingers massaged her nape.
''It's all going to be all right.''

The first tear dampened her cheek. She'd never
cried for Larry. Never cried for herself. But she
wanted to cry for Nick. Because she loved him.

Nick drew her against his chest and wrapped
his arms around her. ''Cry if you want, sweet-
heart. Go on. It'll do you good. You've tried to
be strong for too long.''

''No,'' she sobbed, but she couldn't stop now
that she'd started. Nick's warm embrace undid
her. Completely.

His kisses dried her tears, his mouth found
hers. Their kiss lasted for a long time, sweet, a
homecoming. She'd almost denied herself this.

''I won't let you down, I promise, Rayne. All
I'm going to do is help Silver Island resort and
keep Larry's dreams alive.''

Rayne hugged him tightly.

''I was never going to use you to get the island.
I was attracted to you from the beginning. I didn't
realize that I'd have an attractive woman to con-
tend with as well as a formidable business op-
ponent. And, yes. I'm desperate for you, but I can

wait. Until you're ready. No rush.'' He folded his arms across his chest.

''You mean you won't take off when the deal's done. If I agree, that is.''

''If you don't want me, I'll take off. I'm certainly not a glutton for punishment. So the ball's in your court, Rayne. You can have it all. Silver Island and . . . me.'' Nick's voice cracked a little.

''Tanya pointed out that if . . . if we married, then Silver Island wouldn't go out of the family.''

''True. Is that what you want, us to be married?''

Rayne squeezed her hands tightly together. ''Only if you want it, Nick. I know you saw your parents' marriage go off the rails.''

''It was never on the rails.''

She forced a smile. ''But they're friends now, aren't they?''

''They're at peace, let's say that. Now they can both get on with their lives without so much unfinished business.''

''And I've always wanted a perfect man. So perfect in fact, I never found him. I kept my expectations high so I wouldn't get hurt.''

''And I kept memories of my parents' marriage as a barrier to me ever letting go enough to need someone—as much as I need you, Rayne. I love you, Rayne. It's that simple.''

''And I love you, Nick. It's even simpler.''

They gravitated toward one another and held one another, almost swaying from the force of emotion between them.

Nick said, ''I'll put in as much time to being married to you as I have to my work.''

''I'll second that, Nick.''

''Then our marriage will definitely work, Rayne. You're dedication to this island has driven me crazy.''

''It's been worth it.''

''I'll second that. It's a great island. A dream island. Everyone's idea of a tropical dream.''

For a second Rayne almost thought about her brother, but then she brushed him aside. She'd helped Larry, Tanya, Sean, and Justin. She'd done her best. She'd kept them afloat while they floundered, until they found themselves again. Now it was her turn. . . .